UNDER SUSPICION

Tara Randel

AnniesFiction.com

Books in the Sweet Intrigue series

Betrayal of Trust
Burning Danger
Christmas Peril
Dangerous at Heart
Web of Lies
Deceptive Truths
Fatal Waters
Gathering Storms
Under Suspicion
Guilty Secrets
Hidden Threats
Deadly Tides

Under Suspicion

Library of Congress-in-Publication Data
Under Suspicion / by Tara Randel
p. cm.
I. Title
2021937758

AnniesFiction.com
(800) 282-6643
Annie's Sweet Intrigue™
Series Creator: Shari Lohner
Editor: Lorie Jones

10 11 12 13 14 | Printed in South Korea | 9 8 7 6 5 4 3 2 1

The late afternoon glare reflected off the car hood, bouncing straight into her eyes. Paige Meyers squinted, unsure if the resulting moisture came from the intensity of the Florida sun or the grief that had risen up when she parked in the apartment lot. Either way, it wasn't the best day to have forgotten her sunglasses.

What an emotionally draining afternoon. The funeral had been a touching tribute to Samuel Bishop, her mentor and friend. Samuel had treated her like a second daughter. Without his belief in her, she might still be working dead-end jobs. Instead, he'd hired her as the manager at the historic Poinciana Arms Apartments, located in downtown Peters Cove.

To this day, Paige didn't know what Samuel had seen in a single mother with no experience in apartment management. He had taken a chance, encouraging Paige every step of the way, and over time, she finally started to believe in herself. The job suited her like no other work had, but sometimes it was challenging. It entailed dealing with the various personalities of the tenants, maintaining a three-story building, scheduling work orders, keeping up the grounds, and making a final walk-through at night to check that the lights were off in the laundry room and the basement alarm had been engaged.

Paige could never repay Samuel's kindness, but she'd attended the last farewell to thank the man who had changed everything for her.

Tears blurred her vision. Paige wiped them away, then checked the time. Her sixteen-year-old daughter, Lexi, would be coming home from school soon. She'd better get inside.

Dragging herself from the car, Paige heaved a sigh. She smoothed her dress, hooked her purse over her shoulder, and walked toward the building. Why did she feel like she'd run a marathon? She reasoned it had to be the grief. Life without Samuel would never be the same.

Paige walked from the lot, the low din of traffic sounding from the main thoroughfare two blocks away. The May temperatures were already rising into the eighties at the height of the afternoon.

As soon as Paige entered the courtyard, she felt encased in a cocoon of humidity. The courtyard teemed with mature tropical plants, many blooming with white or pink flowers. The sound of water bubbling from a fountain echoed off the walls. A cement path branched at the fountain, leading to either side of the U-shaped apartment complex.

Despite the heat, she paused to admire the Spanish-style building spread out before her. The building featured aging yellow paint and red shutters. Ornamental balustrades and curving banisters of the two stairwells gave the impression of stepping into a Mediterranean painting. There were twenty-four spacious units in all, and there was hardly ever a vacancy. One of the perks of her job was a major discount on her rent.

Poinciana Arms was home. Here Paige had settled into a comfortable routine of her own making. She had been given the opportunity to provide her daughter with a sense of roots, of permanence. Even if Lexi didn't always make things easy on her.

Paige reminded herself that Lexi was a teenager and it was probably nothing more than a passing phase. At least she hoped so.

A soft meow caught her attention. Paige glanced down and noticed Gus sitting at her feet. The cat was a fixture around the complex. He didn't seem to have an owner, so the residents had adopted him.

"Hey, buddy." Crouching down, she ran her fingers over his soft fur. "Are you hungry? I'll get you a bowl."

Gus meowed as if in response.

Paige hurried along the path with Gus on her heels. Before she reached her destination, Jason Bronson exited the apartment next to hers. She stopped, her heartbeat kicking up a notch at the sudden appearance of the new tenant.

Jason was tall, and he had short black hair. He projected a sense of competency, and Paige wondered if he was former military or law enforcement. There was no question that Jason was handsome. She'd noticed it the moment he'd entered the office to ask about the vacancy. She hadn't been surprised when his references returned with glowing praise. And now she could be bumping into him every day.

Gus trotted over to Jason and rubbed against his ankles.

"Friend of yours?" Jason asked her.

"Gus is a friend to everyone."

"So you're saying I need to stock up on cat food?" he asked as he scratched behind the cat's ears.

"You'll have a buddy for life if you do," Paige answered.

He laughed.

"Are you all settled?" she asked.

"Almost." Jason rolled his broad shoulders. "I moved all the big pieces of furniture in earlier. I have a few boxes left, but that's all."

Paige thought she should offer to help him carry in his belongings, but the funeral had sapped too much of her energy.

"I should have started earlier," he continued. "I forgot how hot it can get by the afternoon."

"Are you a native Floridian?" she asked.

"No, I'm from Michigan, but I've worked in Tampa long enough to know better."

"Thank goodness for air-conditioning."

He grinned. "And iced tea."

They stood in awkward silence. Paige didn't want to brush him off, but her feet hurt in the strappy sandals she rarely wore, and she needed a couple of aspirin to curb her headache.

Jason glanced at her outfit. "Coming from a meeting?"

She ran a hand over the skirt of her black dress. "No, it was a funeral."

His face softened. "I'm sorry."

"Thank you," Paige said around the lump in her throat.

"Can I do anything to help?"

Even through her sadness, she could tell the offer was genuine, not merely given out of politeness. "I should be asking you that question since you're the one moving in."

"I'm only moving stuff," Jason said. "It sounds like you're carrying a weight on your shoulders."

Paige had to admit that he was perceptive. The news of the fatal hit-and-run accident that had taken Samuel's life two weeks ago had come as a horrible shock. She hadn't yet mustered up the emotional strength to think about life going forward without him. It would take time to accept the harsh reality.

With Samuel gone, what did that mean for her future? Paige had no idea what his family would do with the building, especially if the conversations she'd overheard at the funeral were any indication. Not to mention the odd voice mail she'd received from Samuel prior to the tragic accident. He'd been worried about something, but he wouldn't reveal the source. He'd insisted she keep her eyes peeled, whatever that cryptic warning meant. Had it been an actual warning, or had he sensed he'd soon be leaving this world?

Paige pushed away the troubling thoughts. "You're right," she told Jason. "I do feel like I'm carrying a weight on my shoulders. The building owner passed away. Samuel Bishop was my boss and a dear friend." She allowed a slight smile. "Actually, he was more than that. A true father figure."

"It's always tough losing someone who made a major impact on your life."

Had he lost someone close to him? The way his expression closed, she imagined so.

"You must have special memories of your times together," Jason remarked.

Paige blinked. "Excuse me?"

"You said he was a friend," he reminded her. "Mourning him will be difficult, but remembering happier times might cheer you up. At least that's what my grandmother used to say."

She hadn't expected condolences quite like this, especially coming from her new neighbor, but the advice brought a slight smile to her lips. "Yes, I have quite a few special memories."

"How did you meet Samuel?" Jason asked, sounding truly interested.

Paige flashed back to that momentous day. "The manager assigned me to Samuel's table at a trendy restaurant where I worked. One of my part-time jobs." She frowned. "I was a horrible server."

Her other job at the time was a part-time bookkeeper. It had been more to her liking, but it hadn't provided her with enough hours.

"Samuel popped in regularly," Paige continued. "All the waitresses wanted to wait on him because he was kind and generous, but for some reason he always sat in my section. That day was no different, except working too many hours had worn me out."

She sighed. "I wasn't exactly graceful, even on a slow day. Right before my shift ended, I dropped Samuel's plate in his lap. To my surprise, he didn't jump up and demand management fire me. Instead, he laughed and told me I needed to find another line of work. As if I didn't already know this. But his candor was really touching. Before leaving, he handed me his card and asked that I visit his office the following day."

Uncertainty had kept Paige awake all that night. She didn't know this man. Yes, he'd been a steady customer and a generous tipper. If she were honest, she dreaded serving another day. But what were her options? She couldn't rely on her other job to keep them afloat because of the limited hours.

"Well, the next morning, management decided to fire me anyway," she said. "I supposed the mishap with Samuel was the last straw. I didn't want to serve any longer, but losing the job terrified me."

"I assume this story has a happy ending," Jason said with a grin.

Paige surprised herself by chuckling. "It does. When I got home, I remembered Samuel's card and asked a neighbor I trusted to watch my daughter so I could stop by his office. I didn't expect much to come from the meeting, so I was stunned when Samuel offered me a full-time job with benefits. I accepted it on the spot."

"I'm sure he'd want you to focus on those memories," Jason said.

She nodded. Samuel had been the most levelheaded person she knew. He had laughed frequently, bringing joy wherever he went. He'd want Paige and Lexi to march forward, even if it hurt along the way.

Lost in her thoughts, Paige noticed Jason's sympathetic smile and flushed. "I'll treasure the times we shared. Once I get over the shock."

He raised his eyebrows. "Shock?"

She waved her hand in the air between them. "It happened suddenly. A car accident."

Jason flinched. "We might be acquaintances, but since I'm your neighbor now, let me know if I can help in any way."

"That's my job," Paige countered. "But thanks. I might take you up on it."

"I hope you do." His dark-blue eyes grew warm. "I almost forgot to ask. Is there any extra storage available?"

"Yes," she said. "Each unit gets a space in the basement. I can show you later or ask our handyman, Charlie Pollard, to assist you."

Charlie had started working at Poinciana Arms eight months ago. He'd been great from the beginning, but lately he had been acting strangely.

"I'm not in a hurry," Jason said.

"Let me guess," Paige said. "You'll unpack, then repack the extra things you don't need."

"What are you doing, spying on me?"

"You aren't the first renter who has asked me about storage."

His playful expression made him even more handsome. "And here I thought I was special."

She laughed. "If you need anything else, let me know."

"Thanks."

Paige turned when she heard a distinctive bark and rapid footsteps approaching. Mrs. Gertrude Nelson hurried toward them. The spry widow was in her early seventies, and she had short gray hair. Mrs. Nelson cradled her toy poodle, Muffin, who wore a pink bow on her tiny head.

Gus streaked down the sidewalk.

Paige was mere inches away from her door and solitude, but she couldn't escape the duties of her job. She greeted the older woman.

"I'm so glad I caught you," Mrs. Nelson said.

Paige braced herself at the greeting. It usually preceded a complaint. "What can I do for you?"

Mrs. Nelson noticed Jason and smiled. "Who do we have here?"

"A new tenant," Paige said.

Jason stepped forward and held out his hand to the older woman. "Jason Bronson."

"Nice to meet you. I'm Gertrude Nelson." She hugged the toy poodle. "And this is Muffin."

The dog whined. After Mrs. Nelson carefully set Muffin on the ground, the poodle trotted over to Jason and sniffed his shoes.

"You'll love Poinciana Arms," Mrs. Nelson said. "We're like a big, messy family."

Jason reached down to pat Muffin's head. "I'm looking forward to meeting everyone," he said, then nodded to the women. "Please excuse me. I need to get a few more things from my car."

With Jason gone, Muffin inspected the nearby plants.

Mrs. Nelson focused on Paige. "Did you let someone into my apartment last night? I'm sure I mentioned I'd be going out, but did I miss a memo?"

Paige stared at the woman, bewildered. "I didn't allow anyone into your unit. The only person who's been working there is Charlie. Why do you ask?"

"Some of my antiques have been moved around," Mrs. Nelson replied. "I would have asked Charlie about it, but he never came by today."

"I'm sorry," Paige said. "We were at the funeral."

Mrs. Nelson put her hand over her heart. "Oh, my. I forgot that was today."

"Yes, so you can see why Charlie didn't stop by."

"I'm not one to complain," Mrs. Nelson said, "but that pipe leaking in the kitchen has caused more work than I imagined."

"Once you noticed the damage, it meant we had to replace the plumbing and the floor," Paige reminded her.

"I am sorry about that, dear."

"It's fine," Paige assured her. "We were able to catch it before it became a huge issue. I'm glad you told us when you did."

"And I am grateful that you're taking care of it," Mrs. Nelson said.

"So you mentioned some of your antiques were moved," Paige said. "Are you sure?"

Mrs. Nelson huffed. "I think I'd know if things were moved in my apartment. Muffin and I went out last night, and when we came home, she wouldn't stop barking. That's when I noticed my writing table was not precisely centered in front of the window. Plus, the antique writing boxes were moved from one shelf to another."

Paige had seen Mrs. Nelson's unique collection. It contained sloped boxes on which to write correspondence and others to store stationery. Some dated back to the Victorian era, and they were worth a pretty penny.

"Charlie hasn't finished the project," Mrs. Nelson continued, "but I did see another box of flooring in the kitchen."

Charlie had run out of material when he uncovered more damage than originally discovered, which had required multiple visits. He hadn't mentioned that he'd dropped off an additional box when Paige had seen him at the funeral service.

"I'll contact Charlie and see what he says," Paige told her.

"Thank you," Mrs. Nelson said. "You know I hate to be a bother."

Jason returned with a box and a lacrosse stick. "Quick question. Where can I toss the empty boxes?"

"The dumpster is on the other side of the building near the parking lot." Paige pointed. "I think there's a public field south of town if you want to find out about any games."

Jason glanced at his lacrosse stick, then flashed her a smile. "Look at you, anticipating my next question."

"It's what good apartment managers do," Paige said.

"And Paige is wonderful at her job," Mrs. Nelson remarked.

"Good to know," Jason said. "Anything else I should be aware of?"

Paige shrugged. "It's an ordinary apartment building. If you need a repair or the door unlocked for a scheduled service appointment, I always make arrangements beforehand. I can also take package deliveries if you don't want parcels left outside your door."

"Sounds like normal operating procedure," he said.

"We should get home," Mrs. Nelson said, then turned to Paige. "Would you please remind Lexi that she's babysitting Muffin tomorrow afternoon?"

"I'm sure she hasn't forgotten," Paige said, "but I'll check with her."

"Thank you." Mrs. Nelson picked up Muffin, who let out an affronted yip. The woman said goodbye and walked away.

Jason grinned. "Babysitting?"

"Don't worry," Paige said. "Mrs. Nelson's request is normal. Everyone around here helps one another."

He winked at her. "Then I can't wait to meet the rest of the tenants."

She went still, taken aback by his wink. When was the last time a man had winked at her? If ever? And why did her stomach flip at his smile? She ignored her pleased reaction. *Act like a professional,* she reprimanded herself.

Muffin's barking and Mrs. Nelson's hushes filtered down the open breezeway.

"Welcome to life at Poinciana Arms," Paige said.

With a chuckle, Jason waved and stepped into his apartment.

Glad to finally be alone, Paige pulled her phone from her purse and dialed Charlie's number. He'd said he would follow her to the apartment complex after they left the funeral together, but she hadn't seen him yet.

The call went straight to voice mail, so she left a message. "Hey, Charlie. I'm back at the building. Mrs. Nelson is waiting for you. I thought you were right behind me. Call me if there's a problem."

Paige hung up, a bit annoyed. It always bothered her when tenants informed Charlie of a problem in their apartment, but he didn't fill her in on their requests. She had a strict and practical system that worked well, as long as Charlie alerted her. When tenants stopped him in the walkways, he'd forget to remind them that they needed to make arrangements through her first. Usually Charlie worked with her, but lately he'd been unreliable. He'd been late for work more than once, and he didn't always finish a job on the first visit. It wasn't like him, so what was going on?

She suddenly thought of Samuel's warning in his last voice mail to her. Between the weird caution before his death and Charlie falling down on the job, Paige felt overwhelmed. She shook her head, scolding herself for reading too much into nothing.

Paige decided to text Charlie, doubling her attempts to contact the handyman. She quickly typed out her message, then sent it.

Her finger lingered over the device, and she found herself pulling up Samuel's number. How sad that she wouldn't be able to call him, hear his voice whenever she wanted. She tapped an icon, and her saved messages came up. She listened to his last voice mail, her throat growing tight when she heard his dear voice.

"Sorry I missed you, Paige. I wanted to touch base." An urgency had sharpened his tone. "I need to attend to some business, but there are some things going on. We should sit down and talk. I don't want to worry you, but please keep your eyes peeled around the property. I'll stop by later and explain."

But she'd never seen him alive again.

As his plea to be alert repeated in her head, Paige wondered why Samuel had warned her. He'd never been overly dramatic. In fact, he'd been quite the opposite—calm and cool even in the hardest times. What had been bothering him? With a pang of sadness, she realized she'd never know.

With that sorrow came the realization that she might very well be searching for another job if Samuel's family decided to sell the property. What would become of the warm home she and Lexi had created?

Her heart sank as a gloomy cloud hung over the future.

Once Paige stepped into the quiet confines of her apartment, she heaved a sigh of relief. The cool interior greeted her, a solace after the harsh sunlight. She dropped her purse and phone on the counter and kicked off her shoes, replaying the conversation with Jason in her head. He seemed to possess a deep sense of compassion.

She believed her handsome new neighbor would fit right in with the rest of the wonderful tenants. Most were working professionals, about half had children, and the rest were retirees. It was an excellent mix that kept things lively. Holidays were a family affair, which Paige always enjoyed.

Samuel had given her a remarkable gift in this job.

Speaking of which, she needed to go to the office and check if any calls had come in. Dreading the final goodbye to Samuel, she'd forgotten to call the answering service to have the calls transferred to her cell. The idea of walking a few doors down to log complaints drained her, so she flopped into the comfy armchair instead, fighting the headache building behind her temples.

Since Samuel's unexplained voice mail and the announcement of his death, Paige had been on edge. She couldn't shake the odd sensation of being watched. Had she missed something obvious? Every noise she heard in the darkness made her jumpy, and she stayed awake late into the night.

Now those qualms were magnified by Mrs. Nelson's claim that someone had been inside her apartment. The tenants were all very nice. They didn't break into one another's homes. Were Mrs. Nelson's concerns legitimate?

Paige wondered what to do now. She'd recently changed the code to the basement door because she'd been feeling uneasy. There were also security cameras on the premises. She'd viewed the footage in recent days, but nothing unusual stood out. Did she need to get more cameras installed?

Her phone pinged. After the events of today, the exhaustion kept her from retrieving it. She thought it was probably Charlie, answering her text.

She enjoyed a few more minutes of silence, then rose and picked up the phone. Sure enough, Charlie apologized and promised to be on the property tomorrow.

Paige understood Charlie's need for a few hours alone after the funeral. If her emotions were this close to the surface, Charlie most likely felt the same way. She texted back an answer, deciding to cut him some slack. Wouldn't she love to crawl into bed and pull the covers over her head if she had that option?

Lexi would be home any minute. Paige needed to focus on her daughter instead of her troubling thoughts.

The coolness of the tile floor soothed her bare feet as Paige shuffled into the kitchen to pour a tall glass of iced tea. Glass in hand, she wandered around the living room. A few of Lexi's class notebooks littered the coffee table, alongside the novel Paige had started reading. She'd brightened the navy couch with pops of colorful pillows, adding a cheerful patterned blanket over the back of the matching armchair. An area rug covered the floor.

Paige still wanted to hug herself with joy whenever she took a moment to soak up the cozy living space she'd created. She'd allowed Lexi to add suggestions, but her daughter had mainly wanted to set up her bedroom in her own unique way, so Paige had given her free rein.

But what if Paige lost her job? Would her ex-husband, Kevin, insist Lexi come live with him in Georgia? Paige couldn't bear the thought of being separated from her daughter. The idea was so painful it dug right down to the marrow of her bones. No, she'd fight with everything in her to keep this job. No one would take her home—or her daughter—away from her.

She paced to the window that overlooked a grassy area curving from the building to the side street. All in all, Poinciana Arms took up almost a block of a relatively quiet neighborhood. A few cars passed by, and her thoughts returned to Mrs. Nelson. Was the woman imagining things?

Paige had never had a tenant insist that someone had been in her apartment without permission. Paige and Charlie were the only two employees on the premises, and she scheduled all visits by outside workers and made sure the tenants were informed.

Mrs. Nelson had never been forgetful before, but there was a first time for everything. Should Paige tell Charlie? Especially after Samuel's message? Had Samuel worried that the complex might be in some kind of danger? Why hadn't he told her outright instead of leaving her with worries?

The thoughts running circles in her mind made her dizzy. Paige went to her bedroom and changed out of her dress into a T-shirt and jeans. In light of Mrs. Nelson's accusation, maybe she'd take a walk around the property and see if anything was out of place. The one recent mishap had been an electrical glitch in the parking lot gate. It was simply a malfunction, right?

Nerves taut, she cut through the living room as her phone rang. She grabbed it from the counter as she passed by. It was Mason Trembly, Samuel's longtime accountant. She picked up.

"I'm sorry to bother you," Mason said, "but you left the funeral gathering before I had a chance to speak to you."

"It was overwhelming," Paige said, "so I slipped out."

"That's completely understandable."

She heard the gravity in his reply, which reassured her that she wasn't alone in her grief. "Is there an issue you need to discuss?" Normally, Mason called about quarterly reports. Had she missed a deadline or some other tax matter?

"There's something I need to tell you," he said.

Paige winced. That didn't sound promising. "What is it?"

"I apologize for having to do this." Mason paused. "I'll be initiating an appraisal of the building within the week."

"An appraisal?" she repeated. "May I ask why?"

"Samuel started negotiations with a real estate firm expressing interest in purchasing Poinciana Arms," he explained.

Shock rooted her to the floor. "What? He never mentioned it to me."

"All I know is that he told me he had plans for the property," he said. "A future sale."

Samuel had never once referred to a future sale. Why would he sell? He loved this property. He had a few other properties in town, but Poinciana Arms had always been his favorite. Did his last phone call have anything to do with this?

"I appreciate the update," Paige said, trying to keep emotion out of her voice. "I find it hard to believe that Samuel would be interested in selling and not inform me. He was honest about everything regarding the property."

"I'm sure he was," Mason said. "But the building and the land are worth a great deal of money. With all the new construction projects modernizing downtown, developers would naturally vie for that piece of land. Samuel was aware of it."

Samuel had planned to sell the property to allow construction of another high-rise building? He'd commented more than once that the new developments were ruining the small-town charm the Peters family had fostered when they established the town many years ago. No, this didn't make sense.

"You know how Samuel felt about selling out to developers," she said.

"Anyone can change their mind when enticed by a profitable offer."

Paige dropped onto the stool beside the counter. Could money have motivated Samuel? He had wealth. And while he'd always kept an eye out for new investments, he wasn't greedy. The old apartment building needed constant repairs, but to sell so it could be torn down and replaced? No, it still didn't sound right.

"I know this comes as a surprise," Mason said gently, as if trying to soften the blow. "Samuel and the investor were in the beginning stages of negotiations. Perhaps he didn't want to burden you until he'd come to a concrete decision." He cleared his throat. "Anyway, consider this a courtesy call. We'll discuss future matters at a different time."

She could barely speak as he signed off.

"Samuel, were you truly going to sell?" Paige asked the empty room.

What would happen if a sale took place? She had hoped that she'd keep managing the building. If Samuel left the property to a family member who had no connection to it, who could easily sell his legacy, she would have to update her résumé for another job.

Paige flashed back to the conversations after the funeral. She'd been dreading the service, but it had been upbeat, a celebration more than a goodbye. She hadn't wanted to attend the gathering for friends and distant relatives afterward, but she'd stopped by to show support and offer her condolences to his family.

It had gone well until Samuel's nephew, Bennett Calhoun, started complaining about his inheritance. Some kind of family history simmered there, and it wasn't exactly civil from what she'd heard from Samuel. The biting dialogue made her angry. No one was perfect, but Samuel hadn't even come close to being a villain. Refusing to listen to any more attacks on her friend, she'd said her goodbyes and left.

Paige whispered a quick prayer, hoping this turned out to be a big misunderstanding. Mason's information had to be wrong. Even so, who would inherit this place? Samuel had no wife or children, so who would inherit his assets? His nephew?

She jumped up and started pacing, her stomach flipping in jerky cartwheels. "Don't panic," she told herself, which didn't pacify her at all.

"Okay, pros to keep the building." Paige spoke out loud, a leftover habit from a childhood when she had to make decisions because her parents weren't around. "Poinciana Arms is historic, a mainstay of old Peters Cove. Major remodeling might be necessary down the road, but right now it's a shining jewel among brand-new high-rise buildings. Is that enough to keep it safe?"

She ran a hand through her dark hair. "Cons. This is a prime piece of real estate. Any developer would scoop it up in a heartbeat."

Samuel had insisted that he'd never sell. He'd even declined offers in the past. Was it possible he had changed his mind without telling her? Was that why he'd been so strange before his death?

Her heart sank. Paige loved it here. The school district was rated one of the best in the area, and the high school was within walking distance to downtown. Where would she and Lexi go? Again, the threat of custody and Lexi going to live with her dad in Georgia lingered in her mind.

"Stop," she ordered herself. "Until I know more, there's no use imagining the worst."

The door opened, and her daughter bounded inside, tossing her school backpack on the dining table. Lexi stopped when she saw her mother, then hesitantly approached, questions in her blue eyes. "Are you okay?"

Paige had wanted Lexi to attend the funeral, but Lexi, heartbroken by Samuel's death, begged to go to school instead. Her sobs had broken Paige's heart, so she had given in. Now she questioned her decision in not having Lexi make a formal farewell.

"I would have loved to have you by my side at the service," Paige admitted. "It's tough being sad all alone."

Lexi's countenance was bleak. "You were always going to be sad."

Paige hugged her daughter, needing a personal touch in that moment. The day had gone from bad to worse, and only Lexi brought her joy in times like these. She pulled back and smoothed her daughter's long, blonde hair. "That's true, but I still missed you."

"I'm home now."

"How was school?" Paige asked, hoping to lighten the somber mood by changing the subject. "Did you pass your literature test?"

"I got an A."

"That's great. Anything else happen?"

Lexi shrugged. "You know, the usual."

"Which doesn't tell me anything," Paige said. "I spoke to Mrs. Nelson. She wanted me to remind you that you're on Muffin duty tomorrow."

"I didn't forget," Lexi said.

"That's what I told her." Paige went to the kitchen and rinsed out her glass. "Any plans for the weekend?"

Silence.

Paige turned around to find Lexi removing papers from her backpack. Lexi wore an uncertain expression that reminded Paige of her as a little girl when she'd been joyful and not so single-minded.

"I stopped by Mrs. Kelly's antique shop to ask for an application," Lexi said. "I heard through a friend she's hiring part-time help."

Blowing out a breath, Paige tried not to react in a way that would make Lexi feel defensive. "We've had this conversation before. You know I'd rather you focus on your schoolwork."

"I'm getting good grades in my classes," Lexi assured her. "And besides, the school year is nearly over. I'd work during summer break."

Paige couldn't argue. Besides visiting her father, Lexi's schedule was open.

"You know Mrs. Kelly," Lexi continued. "She has lots of cool antiques in her place. I could learn a lot."

Lexi was interested in history, and Mrs. Kelly's store would be a logical place to start a lifelong love, if Paige were to agree.

"What else am I going to do this summer?" Lexi persisted. "Dad hasn't given us the dates for my visit. Watching Muffin from time to time isn't a real job."

"You can help me around the property," Paige suggested.

Lexi rolled her eyes.

Feeling the headache from earlier ramping up, Paige said, "I'll think about it."

A thundercloud passed over Lexi's features. "If Dad were here, he'd let me get a job."

"I'm not your father, and he's not here."

"But he could be," Lexi said.

It was the same old song and dance. Since the divorce five years before, Lexi had been moody and mad at the world. Paige understood that no child wanted her parents to get divorced. But married life with Kevin hadn't worked out for so many reasons Lexi wasn't aware of. Paige and Kevin had kept the specifics to a minimum. But Lexi missed her father and threw her unhappiness in Paige's face whenever they had a disagreement. Where had her sweet little girl gone?

"How about this," Paige started, thinking of a compromise. "While I'm deciding, you help me clean out Samuel's storage closet in the basement. There's bound to be some cool old stuff down there."

In all honesty, Paige would appreciate not having to go through Samuel's belongings alone. In the week before his death, he had insisted that Paige empty his personal storage unit and move everything to his house. Paige had wondered why Samuel had been suddenly adamant about it. In the three years she'd worked here, she wasn't aware that he had even entered his storage unit. Now what would she do with his belongings?

"I hate the basement," Lexi said. "It's musty and creepy."

Paige agreed that it was creepy. Especially with Samuel's warning to be careful running through her head on a nonstop loop. "I'll pay you," she added, sweetening the pot.

"It's not the same," Lexi said.

"But it's a start."

"Fine," Lexi mumbled. She pulled a book from the backpack. "I'm going outside to do my homework."

In the first year on the job, Paige had added a bench and a table in the courtyard for residents to enjoy the surroundings in the temperate weather. Her daughter went there often to escape Paige.

As Lexi stalked by, Paige touched her arm. "You know I love you. It's my job as your mother to guide you."

"More like ruin my life," Lexi muttered.

Tears that had been hovering all day made an appearance. Paige swiped at them, not wanting to be reminded of her grief over Samuel and a perceived failure as a mother.

Had Paige acted like this at sixteen? Probably not. Her father was a colonel, and he wouldn't have put up with her antics. Neither would her mother, who was also an officer. Paige had mostly been alone and left to her own devices. Always alone. How had she thought that would change with her ex-husband, who also put his job first?

It hadn't, so Paige had thrown herself into the job of single mom, regardless of an unhappy teen. How she wished she could talk to Samuel.

Brushing away another wave of emotion, Paige opened the door and leaned against the jamb. She could see Lexi on the bench. Gus had returned, perched beside her while she idly stroked his fur. Her shoulders were stiff, a clear indication of anger. Was Paige wrong not to let her get a part-time job? The school year would end soon. And Lexi did keep her grades up. Why the hesitation? A job might teach her daughter responsibility and the value of money.

Paige's little girl was growing up and becoming a self-sufficient person. But still, Paige wanted her to study so she could get into a high-quality college. Paige had always wanted the full college experience, but she had only been able to go to a local community college part-time to study bookkeeping. Did she simply want Lexi to have so much more than she'd had? Was she pushing what she'd always longed for on her daughter?

She should have taken an aspirin when she got home. These mental gymnastics were not making the pounding in her head any better.

Massaging her temples, Paige turned to go back inside when the oddest sensation shimmered over her. Chills trickled down her arms. It was the same feeling that had come over her from time to time since Samuel had died. She scanned the area, but she didn't see anything out of the ordinary. Except an angry daughter, which was becoming par for the course.

Paige took a few steps into the courtyard. The rich perfume of the lush foliage usually gave her comfort, but it failed to do so now. From here she could see the street. There was nothing unusual out there—no cars she didn't recognize and no one loitering on the sidewalk.

Crossing her arms, Paige hugged her midsection. Growing up around the military, she'd been taught situational awareness from the time she could walk. She didn't normally jump to conclusions, but she never brushed off her reactions when things didn't feel right. At the moment, an inner warning alerted her. Even though she was unable to pinpoint the source, she couldn't dismiss the warning.

Jason popped into her mind. His deep-blue eyes, steady and comforting. His broad shoulders, ready to take on the world. He seemed more than capable of handling any situation. Was that why he came to mind? Jason had offered to lend a hand if she needed anything. Should she tell him about this apprehension building inside her?

Shaking off her concerns, Paige decided not to bother her new neighbor. But she didn't feel comfortable with her daughter outside. She called out, "How about pizza for dinner?"

Lexi perked up. "With pineapple?"

"Sure," Paige replied. "Why don't you come inside, and we'll order?"

Lexi closed the book and made her way back to the apartment, Gus at her feet.

"If you save some room, maybe we can get ice cream later," Paige added.

"No need to go overboard," Lexi said, but Paige was certain she caught a note of amusement in her daughter's voice. "It still won't keep me from wanting a job."

"Fair enough. How about tonight I simply share a nice dinner with my daughter?" Paige peered down at the cat and realized she still hadn't fed him. "And Gus."

"Sounds good." Lexi walked inside.

With Lexi safely in the apartment, Paige indulged in one last sweeping glance of the courtyard. The disturbing feeling that someone was out there slipped away, but she was sure that someone had been watching the apartment building.

She shivered. Who had been out there? And why?

"Not a great way to start the morning," Jason muttered as he slammed the refrigerator door.

How had he forgotten creamer for his coffee? He wasn't a fan of the black stuff, so he'd have to wait to make coffee until he went to the store. He'd intended to go last night, but he'd fallen asleep on the couch, his muscles sore from hours of lifting. Jason was newly forty, and it hadn't bothered him. Now he realized he needed to get back to the lacrosse field if a day of moving tired him so easily.

After adding creamer to his growing grocery list, he decided to forgo his hit of caffeine for a long run. He changed into a T-shirt and shorts, then grabbed his keys. Errands and unpacking could wait until later. Right now, he needed a break.

As Jason stepped outside and twisted the lock, voices came from his left. He turned to find the attractive apartment manager and a teenage girl. The teenager bore a striking resemblance to Paige. Both carried empty boxes and were dressed in T-shirts, shorts, and sneakers. The teen sported a small, sparkly backpack.

Jason had to admit that Paige had captured his attention. She'd been welcoming and full of information when he'd inquired about the apartment, but yesterday he'd witnessed her grief over the loss of her friend. He'd been moved by her sorrow. For reasons he wasn't ready to explore, he wanted to ease her pain, but he didn't have any comforting words to offer her.

Today Paige wore a ponytail, and her brown eyes were dull, with dark circles marring the skin beneath. He understood grief and the pain, uncertainty, and regret that came with it. Paige was clearly still figuring it all out.

When Paige noticed him, she nearly stumbled, and an attractive shade of pink crept into her cheeks. "Good morning."

Jason nodded in greeting. "Let me guess. This is your daughter, Muffin's babysitter."

"Yes, this is Lexi." Paige motioned to him. "And this is Jason Bronson, our new neighbor."

The teen merely nodded.

"Nice to meet you," Jason said to Lexi, then addressed Paige. "Hope you're feeling better today."

"Nothing a little work won't cure." Paige hitched her shoulders, almost as if trying to convince herself of the old adage.

"Working on a Saturday," Lexi groused. "Everyone gets a day off."

"That would be on Sunday," Paige said with a grin.

"What's the chore today?" he asked.

"We're heading to the basement to clean out a storage closet," Lexi answered in a bored tone.

"It's not that bad," Paige said.

Jason raised his eyebrows. "The same storage area you told me about yesterday?"

"Yes." Paige hesitated. "Why don't you come with us and check out the space? If you're not busy, that is."

"Actually, I happen to be free. I was going for a run, but it can wait." Truth be told, he was more interested in getting to know his neighbor.

"Then follow us," Paige said.

Jason fell into step behind the women as they walked to the far end of the breezeway, stopping before a large door located on the outside of the building.

Paige unlocked the door, then stepped inside, flipped a switch, and tapped a security keypad mounted on the wall.

Once she disengaged the alarm, they descended the illuminated stairway. The temperature dipped, and a blast of musty air greeted him, followed by the humidity that came from a sublevel basement. The walls were lumpy, as if someone had applied stucco over them as an afterthought, and the concrete floor was uneven. By his estimation, the entire space ran the length of the back part of the building.

"Creepy," Lexi muttered under her breath.

"This way," Paige said before stopping under a pull cord. She tugged it, and light flooded the area.

Murky shadows lingered in the corners of the long room. Jason had to admit it was indeed creepy. Clearly the place hadn't been modernized in many years.

Paige set her boxes on the floor. "Sorry for the old-school storage. When we updated the lock system in the complex, Samuel never got around to revamping the units down here."

"It's not a problem," Jason said as he perused his surroundings. He regarded a tall storage unit about the size of an armoire. On the opposite wall, a row of numbered units ran the length of the space. Wire fencing marked off each individual space.

"You're more than welcome to use an empty unit," Paige offered. "You'll need your own lock."

"Sounds good," he said, still studying the space.

"Anytime you need to come downstairs, press the button on the key fob you received when you moved in," Paige continued. "If there's a problem, drop by the office and schedule a time for me or Charlie to unlock the door."

Jason nodded as he passed the full units, then walked into the dim recesses to find one he could claim later. On this opposite end of the basement, he made out the outline of another door. After noting the number of an empty space, he backed up and returned to the women. "I'd be happy to help out."

"Thanks for the offer," Paige said. "But you don't need to do that. We have it covered."

"I insist." He rubbed his hands together. "So, should we divvy up the sorting?"

"No," Lexi said.

At the same time, Paige said, "Yes."

"That was as clear as mud," Jason said with a laugh.

Paige twisted her mouth in a rueful grimace. "As usual, my daughter and I are not on the same page."

"Try the same book," Lexi said.

With a shake of her head, Paige unlocked the closet before her. The thick wood held a patina that spoke to the age of the unit, as compared to the open sections available to the tenants. Paige had to jiggle the tarnished lock to make the key mechanism move. Once it clicked, the entire piece shifted in place.

"Looks like it hasn't been opened in a while," he commented.

"This is Samuel's personal storage unit. To be honest, I've never gone into it." Paige gently removed the key, her other hand cupped below as if she were afraid the entire lock would fall out. "I've been here three years, but only recently did he ask me to clean it out." When she glanced at him, her pretty features were veiled in shadow.

Her troubled expression made the muscle in his jaw flex. Trying to hold back his many questions so he wouldn't make Paige feel worse, he went for the obvious. "Did Samuel want something in particular?"

"Not that he mentioned." Paige opened the doors wide, revealing the closet that was deeper than it was wide and held neatly arranged shelves. "He asked before he died . . ." Her voice wavered, and she placed a hand on the side of the unit as if to steady herself. "He wanted me to sort through his things, then box them up and take them to his house. I guess now I'll wait and see what the family wants to do with his belongings."

"Why bother?" Lexi asked. "Maybe they'll want to toss everything."

"Then we'll be ready." Paige grabbed an empty box off the floor. "Let's get started."

Jason scanned the area around them. "Can I make a suggestion?"

Paige raised one eyebrow.

"Do you have a table?" he asked. "It'll be easier to sort through the items before placing them in boxes."

Paige appeared sheepish. "I should have thought of that. Sorry. Didn't sleep well last night."

"Understandable." It also explained the dark circles under her eyes.

"Just a second." Paige headed to the stairwell. She vanished behind the steps, then backed out again, dragging a long table.

Jason hurried over and lifted the other end of the table.

"Thanks." Paige cleared her throat and began walking.

Her floral perfume wafted his way as they moved, intriguing him even more.

Once they were back at the unit, they lowered the legs and set the table upright.

Paige was quiet as she removed items from the shelves and gently placed them on the table.

Jason couldn't miss the sadness etched into her features.

Across from her mother, Lexi dropped her glittery backpack to the floor beside her feet.

After a few minutes of silence, Paige asked, "Do you work in Tampa?"

He gathered some glassware to place in a box. "Yes. Near the Air Force base."

Paige raised a questioning brow at him.

"I work for a defense contractor," Jason explained.

"So you were in the military?" Paige asked.

"Yes, I was in the Air Force for a long time."

Paige didn't say anything else. Instead, she focused on her work.

"My dad's in the Army," Lexi said as she picked through the knickknacks on the table.

He noticed a pile of the smaller belongings on her right that weren't making it into the box.

"He's stationed in Georgia," Lexi went on. "And my grandparents are stationed in Texas."

"Sounds like a military family," Jason commented, curious why Paige avoided making eye contact with him.

"Except Mom," Lexi added.

He couldn't help noticing that Paige wore no gold band on her ring finger.

Paige's mouth tightened. "Divorced."

The one emphatic word ended the topic, but at least he'd learned he hadn't taken too much notice of a very attractive married woman.

"What's a defense contractor?" Lexi asked as she took some books to place in the box near her elbow.

"The easiest way to explain is that I work on a contract basis for a company that provides products or services to the military or government," Jason replied. "In our case, the company I work for develops cutting-edge technology to help both sectors."

"So, computers and stuff?" Lexi asked.

"Yes, but it's a little more complicated than that."

By Paige's irritated expression, he could tell that she'd recognized the presence of top secret information he wasn't allowed to reveal. He wasn't surprised. After all, Paige knew all about the military.

"That sounds cool. My dad is an MP. He works a lot of hours, but he calls me all the time." Longing came into Lexi's eyes. "I'm going to see him during summer break."

"He'll let us know when he gets his schedule," Paige said, a slight frown wrinkling her brow.

Did she need to reassure Lexi that her dad would make time for her? He understood that minefield. Lexi wasn't the first teen struggling between divorced parents.

As the two talked about summer plans, Jason realized the topic of Lexi's dad was a source of friction between them. He didn't want the direction of the conversation making things awkward, so he changed the subject. "Will your handyman be joining us?"

"No, Charlie has a few other projects to catch up on." Paige checked her watch. "Actually, he should be here by now. Mrs. Nelson will be calling me if he doesn't finish her floor."

"Does he make it a habit of showing up late?" Jason asked.

"Only recently." Paige waved a hand as if brushing off any concern, but traces of frustration remained. "I'm not sure what's going on with him."

"Maybe he's sad about Samuel," Lexi said in a quiet voice.

"Oh, honey." Paige rounded the table and pulled her daughter into a hug.

It touched Jason to see their bond. It was miles from the type of relationships he'd grown up around.

Paige stepped back and cupped her daughter's face. "We'll get through this."

Lexi nodded, then added a few more objects to her growing pile.

Once the emotion had passed, they got back to work. One box was filled with glassware. Jason figured the pieces must have either monetary or sentimental value since they had been locked up. Another box contained antique astronomy tools. He recognized a brass sextant, a vintage naval astrolabe, and a dozen compasses of different sizes. A third box held miscellaneous items, such as a tin of old-fashioned keys and locks, an old cigar humidor, and a tabletop clock. The final box contained a variety of books.

"Samuel must have had an interest in astronomy," he remarked as he studied a compass.

Paige lifted a small telescope and blinked rapidly. "When we first met Samuel, he'd take Lexi and me stargazing. He knew all the constellations and loved pointing them out."

Lexi took the telescope from her mother. "Tell him why."

Paige bit her lip. "Samuel had a daughter, but she died when she was twenty. While Claire was growing up, it had become a passion for both of them. Then Lexi and I showed up, and he had a captive audience. I think he wanted to impart his knowledge as a way of honoring Claire. Imagine his surprise when he mentioned the subject and found we were truly interested."

Lexi smiled. "He should have been a teacher. During our astronomy section in science, I got straight As because of him."

"He sounds like a good man," Jason said.

Paige traced her fingertip over the ornate carving on a silver astrolabe, blinking quickly. "He said we were family."

"And now he's not here," Lexi choked out, then rushed over to the stairs, taking a seat on the bottom step.

Paige sighed. "Maybe we shouldn't have brought up that topic."

He touched her arm, his fingers barely resting on her soft skin. "The grief is always going to be there. Hiding from the memories never makes the process easier."

"I agree. But Lexi has had a lot to handle lately. I hate to see her experiencing so much loss."

"She seems pretty resilient."

Paige smiled. "She is."

By the time Lexi returned, she had managed to pull herself together. She launched right into her hopes for a summer job.

Jason hid a grin. He could tell Lexi was determined to convince her mother whether Paige agreed or not.

"And I'll have my own money," Lexi said. "I won't have to bug you for an allowance."

Paige held up a hand. "I'll think about it."

Lexi pouted as they finished boxing the items. When the closet was empty, they folded the lids of the box tops.

"What now?" he asked.

"I think we should store Samuel's things in my office." Paige carefully closed and locked the storage doors. "They'll be safe there. Once I find out his wishes for the property, we can decide what to do next."

Jason glanced around to make sure they hadn't left anything behind when he noticed Lexi slipping a few items from the pile into her backpack. Oblivious to his attention, she kept her gaze glued to her mother's back.

What did Lexi need with an old key, a glass paperweight, and a compass? And why didn't she ask her mother if she could take a few mementos of the man they both loved? Her actions struck him as furtive, which piqued his interest.

Lexi quickly zipped up the front flap with the items inside. Her eyes went wide when she finished her task and saw Jason watching her. She stared at him with a mixture of guilt and defiance for a moment. When Jason didn't rat her out, she said, "I'm going upstairs to call Tina. We're supposed to hang out before I watch Muffin."

"That's fine, but let's get lunch first." Paige faced Lexi, clearly unaware of her daughter's actions. "Ready?"

"No, I need to run. I'll eat with Tina." Lexi grabbed her backpack and took off.

Jason found Lexi's actions extremely suspicious. His years in covert ops had taught him not to ignore his inner voice. Although he'd retired from that world, the innate sense never went away. He wouldn't allow it to.

"Thanks for all your help," Paige said. "I didn't mean to put you to work."

"It was my pleasure."

"Why don't you join me for lunch? I ordered two sandwiches, and I'm not hungry enough to eat them both myself." She sent him a sheepish grin. "It's the least I can do for taking up your entire morning."

Pleasantly surprised, he asked, "You wouldn't mind?"

"Not at all."

Jason thought about his original plans. A run and a trip to the store could always wait until later. He didn't want to pass up the opportunity to spend more time with Paige. "Then I accept. After we eat, I'll help you lug these boxes upstairs."

They made their way up the stairs. Paige closed and secured the door behind them.

The heat of the day drifted into the breezeway, the air fresh and clean in contrast to the damp basement.

Paige tucked a loose strand of hair behind her ear. "I hope Lexi didn't make you uncomfortable by bringing up her dad. Chalk it up to way too much information from a chatty teenager."

He was more interested in what Lexi was up to. Why had the teenager taken Samuel's belongings? Was it her way of holding on to a man who had become family? But why the secrecy? Surely her mother would have understood. "I don't think I can name any family who doesn't engage in a bit of drama now and then."

Paige shot him a knowing look. "Sounds like you speak from experience."

Jason nodded. "A product of divorced parents. It wasn't easy, but at least I had my sister to get through the tough times."

A sister who had acted out. Alyssa was a kleptomaniac, and her ways of coping were a constant source of embarrassment to the family, especially for a control freak father who couldn't stop his daughter's habit. His mother lived in denial. Jason hadn't truly understood Alyssa's issues until he went to college. He worked with his sister to get professional help, but by then, the damage had already been done.

"Does it ever get easier?" Paige asked.

"I suppose it does in time. Each case is different. You clearly love your daughter."

"I do. And so does her father." Her voice grew fierce. "Lexi is the most important thing in my life. I'd do anything for her."

Including cover for her? Much like his mother had done for his sister? Except Paige hadn't seen her daughter's actions.

Despite his unexpected attraction to Paige, Jason had a hunch he needed to be observant around the mother and daughter in the future. Maybe it was a fluke. But Lexi chose to be sneaky, and that bothered him.

His many years in covert ops and his time spent bailing his sister out of one mess after another had taught him that people weren't always what they seemed.

What were his new neighbors' secrets?

After a lunch of sandwiches and potato chips from a local shop around the corner, Paige collected the wrappers and started to clean up the kitchen.

Jason carried the empty glasses to the sink and rinsed them out.

"So why Poinciana Arms?" Paige finally asked the question that had been burning inside all during lunch.

"When I was stationed in Tampa, my friends and I often drove to Peters Cove for dinner," Jason answered. "We liked the small-town vibe. On one of our many trips, we walked through the neighborhood and passed by this building. I kept thinking about this place, and when I needed to find a new apartment, I took a chance and called."

She leaned against the counter. "You're really lucky. Normally we don't have vacancies, but one of the tenants had to move because of a job transfer."

"I figured it was probably a long shot, but I'm glad I gave it a try."

Disconcerted by this attractive man standing in her apartment, Paige tried to come up with something to say. She was interested in getting to know Jason, but she didn't have time for a relationship, especially now with the future so uncertain. For all she knew, she and Lexi might be searching for a new place of their own soon.

"Whatever you're thinking, it can't be that bad," he said.

She jerked her head in his direction. "What?"

"You're wearing a very focused look."

Paige hoped she wasn't blushing. "I have a lot on my mind."

"Related to work?"

His question reminded Paige of her conversation with Mason Trembly. Couldn't he wait until Samuel's last will and testament was revealed before moving forward with a business deal? The respectful thing to do would be to wait until after the reading so the family members could make their wishes known. Shaking off the confusion and fear that had resulted from his call, she rolled her shoulders and met Jason's unwavering gaze.

"Why don't we go downstairs for those boxes?" Paige suggested when the silence grew heavy.

Jason shot her a devastating grin. "You're good at changing the subject." He held up his hand. "Sorry. I don't mean to pry."

"It's okay. Samuel's passing has put a lot of things up in the air."

"I've found that keeping busy usually helps when I have a lot on my mind."

She definitely needed a distraction. Between the possible sale of the building and the feeling of being watched yesterday, she'd tossed and turned last night. She wondered if Samuel's relatives were keeping tabs on their future investment. And what about the claim by Mrs. Nelson that someone had been in her apartment?

Paige pushed away from the counter. "You're right. Let's get to work."

They left her apartment and went down into the basement again.

Paige put her hands on her hips. "Since Lexi abandoned us, we'll need to make two trips."

Jason motioned to the stairs. "After you."

With a grunt, Paige lifted a box and carried it upstairs. At her office, she set it down to dig her keys from her pocket and open the door. The big space contained desks for her and Charlie, a few filing cabinets, and a table for a printer and other office equipment. She tossed the keys on her desk.

Jason entered with two boxes. "Where do you want these?"

"You can put them under the window." Paige brushed her hair from her eyes, then hauled her box over and set it down on the floor next to his. "Ready for round two?"

"There's only one box left," he said. "I'll get it."

A few minutes later, he returned with the last box and added it to the stack.

"Now you're free for the rest of the day," she remarked as they left the office.

"I didn't mind helping."

"And I can't thank you enough," Paige said, closing the office door behind them.

Brian Larson from the third floor strolled over to them. A clerk at a nearby tech store, he was in his late twenties with shaggy blond hair.

Paige introduced Jason and Brian.

The men shook hands and exchanged a few pleasantries.

"I wanted to thank you for letting the repairman into my apartment the other day," Brian told Paige. "I had to work late, and I would have missed him otherwise." He shook his head. "Although it's weird because the Internet is still glitchy."

Paige felt the blood drain from her cheeks. "I waited until six, but no one showed up. I assumed you rescheduled the appointment."

Confusion crossed Brian's features. "Really? I figured you let him in since we'd made arrangements beforehand."

"No, I'm sorry." She swallowed hard, trying to act normal, but she felt Jason watching her. *Pull it together.* "I guess that explains why the connection isn't working."

Brian pulled out his phone. "I should call." He paused, then sent her a sheepish grin. "I have a message asking to reschedule. I must have overlooked it."

Paige felt a huge wave of relief. "If you still need me to let the repairman in, let me know."

"I'll get back with you after I reschedule." Brian frowned. "It's weird. I could have sworn someone was in the apartment."

She felt a chill down her spine. "Why would you think that?" she asked, trying to keep her voice even.

"I found the modem on the floor, and I usually keep it on my desk," Brian replied. "But I did some rearranging recently, so I must have set it aside and forgotten about it."

Paige wasn't so sure. It seemed like too much of a coincidence for Brian and Mrs. Nelson to have a similar story. Could the same thing really have happened twice?

"Sorry I bothered you for nothing," Brian said. "I'm going to check my mail. Talk to you later." With a wave, he took off for the mailboxes located on the sidewalk near the street.

"Do you have ghosts in this place?" Jason asked after Brian was gone.

She faced him. "What?"

"Service guys who let themselves in and then don't actually fix anything?" he asked. "Come on. There has to be an explanation."

"And you think it's a ghost?" Paige laughed, but it sounded fake. "No. Every once in a while, the tenants and I get our signals crossed. It's happened to Charlie before too."

"So I shouldn't be worried?"

"Of course not," she replied with more conviction than she felt.

Jason didn't say anything as he watched her intently.

Paige didn't like the doubt reflected in his eyes. She needed to change the subject before he asked any more questions. By his determined expression, she assumed he wasn't ready to give up. "It'll get straightened out," she said, hoping she sounded casual. "When you're ready to claim that storage space, let me know."

Without waiting for a response, Paige hurried to her apartment. Once inside and out of Jason's sight, she placed shaking hands against the door and gulped in steadying breaths.

All her worries came crashing down on her. Was someone lurking around the building and trespassing in tenants' apartments? The idea horrified her.

Paige needed to discuss her concerns with someone. With Samuel gone, who could she talk to about all this uncertainty? Of course, she would never burden or frighten her daughter with any of this. Paige told herself that sorrow, a lack of sleep, and fear over the future were most likely causing her to overreact. No, it was better to keep her qualms to herself.

Even so, Paige felt a sense of dread that she couldn't ignore. To her surprise, she considered talking to Jason. But if she confided in him, he might wonder what he'd gotten himself into by moving here. Besides, Jason was still a stranger to her.

Despite her growing panic, Paige had to admit that she had a high comfort level with Jason, considering they'd just met. It had little to do with his attractiveness and everything to do with the way he commanded a situation.

Could she really trust Jason? Or would confiding in him be a terrible mistake?

Jason watched Paige practically run to her apartment. He hadn't missed the way she blanched when Brian asked about the mysterious repairman. He didn't believe in coincidences. If he had to guess, Paige didn't either. That was probably why she took off instead of continuing their conversation.

Deciding to get cleaned up, he headed toward his apartment. On the way, he found Brian sorting through his mail.

On impulse, Jason stopped the young man. "Hey, do you have a minute?"

"Sure." Brian glanced around, then leaned closer. "Do you want the scoop on the building?"

"Actually, yes," Jason said. Going behind Paige's back was pretty low, but she hadn't been forthcoming about what was happening. He had no other choice but to get information elsewhere. "Is there anything I should be aware of?"

Brian raised his eyebrows. "What do you mean?"

"You know, gossipy neighbors." Jason shrugged. "People who borrow things and never return them."

"A couple of tips," Brian said with a grin. "Only park in the spot with your unit number. Otherwise, your neighbors will be in an uproar."

"Parking is serious around here?"

"Even small towns have limited parking," Brian responded. "The owner bought the lot next door so we'd have extra room, but the older folks don't like leaving their cars in the grass. Personally, I don't care." He snapped his fingers. "Oh, don't lose your key card for the gate. It takes a while to get a new one."

"Got it," Jason said. "Anything else?"

"Watch out for Muffin. She yaps a lot."

"I had the pleasure of meeting her yesterday."

"She's a sweet dog, but sometimes her barking can get on your nerves. Mrs. Nelson is great, but she tends to spoil Muffin." Brian pointed out the mailboxes and mentioned the community grill out back.

Jason thanked Brian for all the information, even though Paige had already told him about the amenities when he'd signed the lease. It was time to ask the deeper questions. "So, is it safe around here?"

"Safe? Huh." Brian seemed to mull it over. "It must be because I never stop to think about it."

Jason thought that wasn't the best recommendation, but he kept the comment to himself. "Does Paige keep up with security?"

"Yeah. She's really picky about letting people into our apartments. Or holding on to keys and stuff. But she makes sure to be available whenever you need her." Brian cocked his head. "Why are you asking? Did something happen? Paige did act weird when I asked her about the repairman."

"I'm simply getting a lay of the land," Jason said, "and I figured you might have some answers."

Brian puffed up. "Yeah, I do. I've been living here for four years."

"I appreciate it." Jason leaned in, sounding conspiratorial to elicit more information. "It sounds like Paige has a lot on her plate with letting repairmen into apartments. Are you sure you moved your things around?"

"I always rearrange and forget where I put stuff," Brian said nonchalantly. "I didn't mean to make Paige feel bad."

"I think she takes her role as manager seriously."

"She doesn't need to worry," Brian said. "I mean, yeah, she gets sidetracked, but she's a competent manager."

"Sidetracked?" Jason repeated.

"Her daughter. There's always some drama going on with Lexi."

Jason's mind flashed to Lexi slipping Samuel's belongings into her backpack. "Anything I should be concerned about?"

"Nah. Just the usual teenage stuff."

After they said their goodbyes and Brian walked away, Jason returned to his apartment, wondering what was going on. He had read the confusion in Paige's expression when Brian had mentioned that his modem had been moved. Paige might have daughter drama, but did that translate into trouble in the building? If it did, would she tell Jason? If he were in her shoes, he'd keep his concerns locked up tight until they got to know each other better.

He'd clearly stumbled into something with both Paige and Lexi. While Paige was clearly scared, Lexi acted as if she was trying to hide something from her mom. Were the two instances related?

His earlier hunch convinced him that something suspicious was going on with mother and daughter.

Should Jason investigate or mind his own business? He feared that whatever he did, something awful was about to happen.

After taking a few minutes to pull herself together, Paige realized she really wanted to go back and talk to Jason. It took everything in her power not to do so. What would she say to the man? That odd things were happening around the complex? That the nice building he'd moved into had suddenly become a plot from a mystery novel? No, she needed to see what happened next before getting him involved.

Next? Paige let out a groan at the thought.

Noise from the television finally filtered into her brain. She glanced around the living room. Lexi wasn't around.

"Lex?"

No answer.

Paige crossed the room and grabbed the remote to turn down the TV.

"Hey, I was listening to that," Lexi said as she exited her room.

"You had the volume up so loud that you didn't hear me when I called."

Lexi shrugged.

"Are you going to Mrs. Nelson's apartment?" Paige asked as she tidied the coffee table.

"Yeah. I hope she won't be gone long."

"Why?" Paige paused to study her daughter. "Do you have plans later?"

"I do."

Paige frowned, wondering what Lexi's plans were. "I thought you already saw Tina."

Lexi sat down on the armchair and put on her beat-up sneakers. "We hung out for a while."

Paige recognized her daughter's attempt to evade a question. "Was Tina the only one there?"

"No. It was a group from school."

"Do I know them?" Paige asked, wary.

"They're from my class," Lexi answered.

Familiar with that tone, Paige stopped pressing. She wouldn't get anywhere.

"Later we want to go to the park, if that's okay with you."

The waterfront park drew kids in the community like a magnet. The marina and an upscale hotel anchored one end of the block's long grassy park with plenty of mature shade trees. A collection of restaurants, boutiques, and art galleries catered to the tourists. South of the downtown business district, the foot traffic slowed as the area transitioned to the residential district. On the whole, it was a safe place for kids to grow up without worries. An environment where Lexi would develop into an independent woman. Paige wouldn't let her guard down, especially if Kevin started questioning their custody arrangement again. No way could he learn about the events surrounding Poinciana Arms.

"It's fine, but please be careful when you're out," Paige said. "You never know what can happen."

Lexi rolled her eyes. "You're really giving me the speech about strangers?"

Paige might not be able to prove her strong feeling of being watched, but the possibility of Lexi being in danger made her stomach roll, so she wasn't cutting her daughter any slack. "No matter how old you are, it never hurts to be aware of your surroundings or the people you're with, especially since I haven't met them. Hint, hint."

"You've met most of my friends," Lexi argued.

"How many do you have that I haven't met?"

Lexi jumped up. "What is wrong with you?"

"I want to make sure you're all right."

"I'm fine. Pay attention to your own life."

Paige flinched. "What does that mean?"

"Our new next-door neighbor," Lexi answered. "I saw the way you were checking him out."

"What are you talking about?" Paige asked. "He's a nice guy who offered to help us."

Lexi scooped up the sparkly backpack she used as a purse. "If you say so."

"We just met."

"But I can tell you like him."

Paige tilted her head. "Is this about your dad?"

"No." She pouted. "Well, kind of."

"You know your dad and I don't work."

"But you could if you tried," Lexi pleaded.

"We tried. We have different ideas about life." Paige wanted to hug Lexi, but she knew that wouldn't be welcome right now. Paige desperately wanted to resolve this ongoing conflict between them, but it was difficult. "Your dad and I love you more than anything. We'd do anything for you."

"Like get back together?" Lexi asked.

Paige let out a breath. "I'm sorry, but we can't do that."

"Yeah, that's what I thought." Lexi put her backpack over her shoulder and stormed out of the apartment, slamming the door.

"Good talk," Paige muttered.

She wandered to the window. Lexi wasn't completely wrong. She couldn't deny her interest in Jason. It had been a long time since she'd been attracted to a man. Maybe he didn't share her feelings. Did she want to be humiliated? And then there was his stint in the Air Force. Could she get involved with a retired military man? She'd had her fill of that lifestyle, and she didn't want to go back.

Samuel had never pushed her. His belief in her was the one thing Paige had always appreciated about him. He'd make a request, whether about managing the building or finding a restaurant where they might dine with Lexi, and let her come up with her own conclusions. It made them a first-rate team. So much of her life prior to coming to Poinciana Arms had been spent doing what other people wanted and following rules that suited them.

Pack up. We're moving to a new base.

Don't get too close to those friends. We'll be traveling soon.

Sure, you can work after we're married. Except you can't because I'm up for a promotion.

Paige was happier here than any of the myriad locations she'd lived in her thirty-eight years. Military life hadn't been for her, not as a child or a wife. She'd learned to take care of herself when her parents and husband put the military first, but they'd never recognized that she could make her own decisions. When the Army had transferred Kevin across the country, Lexi would have been moved to yet another school. At the time, her daughter had struggled with her lessons. Lexi needed stability and consistency.

Paige and Kevin had argued about it. In the end, Paige left him, realizing that her dissatisfaction stemmed from more than not wanting to move again. She finally admitted that she couldn't live with him. Being on her own couldn't be as disappointing as being married to the wrong man. She'd been terrified, wondering what she'd been thinking, until she landed this job. Since then, both Paige and Lexi had prospered, even though Lexi still questioned why Paige wouldn't reconcile with Kevin. How could Paige explain that to a teen who wished her parents were still together? No wonder Lexi's moods swung so frequently.

Paige could never have dreamed of living anywhere better than this Florida town. But that could change. What if the strange events going on somehow caused her to lose Lexi?

And now Samuel was dead, and Paige didn't know what to do next.

It seemed security was only an illusion.

Rubbing her hands up and down her arms, she couldn't deny the fear that was growing inside her every day. It had started with Mason's surprising phone call about selling the building and the feeling that someone was watching her. No, her fear went back even farther. Samuel had warned her to keep her eyes open. And Paige could sense that Samuel's nephew was planning to make waves regarding the will.

What would it all mean in the end? Losing her job? Her home? Her daughter? Everything she held dear?

The shrill ring of the phone made her jump a foot off the floor. Whenever she left the office, she had calls forwarded here.

Pressing her hand to her chest to calm her pounding heart, Paige hurried to the landline and snatched up the receiver. "Poinciana Arms. How may I help you?"

"Don't get too comfortable," a muffled voice said. "You won't be at Poinciana Arms much longer."

"Who is this?" Paige asked, her voice cracking. "What are you talking about?"

"You'll be leaving soon. Very soon."

With trembling fingers, Paige hung up. The unidentifiable voice was intimidating. Surely, the caller had made a mistake and had meant to frighten someone else.

But what if it was intentional?

On top of the prickly sensation of being watched, now Paige had to worry about prank calls? Yes, it had to be a prank, she told herself, despite the sinking feeling in the pit of her stomach.

She headed to her bedroom when her cell phone rang. Paige went to the counter, then slowly picked up the device and checked the screen. *Unknown caller.* With mounting dread, she swiped the answer button. "Hello?"

"You'll be leaving soon, whether you like it or not."

"Who is this?"

"Someone who is keeping an eye on you."

The shower had cleared Jason's head. He decided to ask Paige why she took off after the conversation with Brian. If anything, he wanted to convince her that she needed a friend.

Jason left his apartment and went next door. As he raised his hand to knock, the door suddenly burst open.

Paige gasped and stopped short. "I'm sorry. I didn't know anyone was out here."

"I didn't mean to bother you." He studied her ashen face. "Are you all right?"

She grimaced. "Does an unhappy teenage daughter count?"

"Are you sure that's all?" Jason asked. He could tell that she wasn't joking.

"Let's try this again," Paige suggested. She straightened her shoulders and smoothed her features. "I'm okay. So what can I do for you?"

"I was wondering if I could talk to you for a few minutes," he said. "But I see that you were leaving, so I can come back later."

"I thought I'd go for a walk, but it can wait." She backed up and held the door open. "Come in."

Jason followed her inside, caught in the wake of her floral perfume.

In the middle of the living room, Paige asked, "Does your checking up on me have anything to do with your job?"

He reared back. "What does my job have to do with anything?"

"If you're working on cutting-edge technology, I'm assuming you have a security clearance, and that would explain all your questions."

"I knew you'd pick up on that," Jason said.

She nodded. "I grew up in the military."

"From your tone, I'm guessing you didn't like it."

"I wouldn't say I disliked it," Paige replied. "It simply wasn't the right fit for me. My parents thrived on the culture, but I found it stifling."

"I get it," he said. "It's not for everyone."

"My parents never knew why I was uncomfortable with military life," she said. "Samuel understood me better than my own folks. He believed in me and trusted my judgment." She bit her lip. "It sounds crazy, but he *saw* me."

"That doesn't sound crazy," Jason assured her. "It sounds like he knew the real Paige."

"I wish I'd figured myself out before I married Lexi's father," Paige remarked with a sigh. "Although I did get her out of the deal, and I love her to pieces."

He smiled. "Seems like a fair exchange."

"Sorry I snapped at you. Please have a seat." She motioned to the armchair and took a seat on the nearby couch. "Do you mind if I ask why you retired?"

Jason sat down on the comfortable chair. "I was ready for a change."

She nodded. "I've been there."

"I didn't have a Samuel in my life," he continued. "A buddy started the company I work for now and talked me into joining him. Since I'm always up for a challenge, I couldn't resist."

"I'm glad you had that opportunity," Paige said. "Now, what did you want to talk to me about?"

His lips quirked. "It was nothing related to the apartment. Not that you haven't been incredibly helpful in that regard."

"You just moved in, so it'll take you some time to get into the rhythms of the building. But I hope I've answered all your practical questions."

"What about the impractical ones?"

She sat up. "Why do I feel like this is about to become an interrogation?"

Jason leaned forward and rested his elbows on his jean-clad knees. "It's a fatal flaw of mine. I need answers to everything." With Paige, it came from more than his nature of relentless questioning. A mysterious force drew him to her, and he needed to unravel the mystery of this growing attraction. "It's gotten me in hot water more than a few times. Why should today be any different?"

Paige glanced away.

Jason realized that she wasn't in the mood for levity, so he plunged ahead. "When Brian mentioned that he felt like someone had been in his apartment, you turned pale."

She waved him off. "You're imagining things."

"Am I? Then how do you explain the circles under your eyes?"

"I already told you that Samuel died," Paige said. "And I haven't been sleeping well."

He ran a hand over his short hair. "We hardly know each other, but I sense something is going on. I can read it on your face."

"It's nothing."

"I'd like to help if you'll let me," Jason said, keeping his voice kind and even. "You're obviously under a lot of stress. I'm concerned about you."

"Well, don't be," she said. "I'm more than capable of dealing with my issues and handling this building."

"I didn't say you weren't. But—"

Before he could finish, an alarm wailed from somewhere on the property.

"What's that?" he asked.

Paige stared at him in horror. "The basement alarm."

Paige couldn't believe that the alarm had gone off. What was going on? Was someone trying to break into the basement?

Both Paige and Jason jumped up from their seats and rushed out of her apartment.

As they ran toward the basement, Paige was relieved that Jason charged along right beside her. She didn't have time to contemplate the hard line of his mouth. Nor did it concern her to see his jaw tighten. Strangely enough, his take-charge attitude bolstered her entrance into the unknown.

As they rounded the corner, she gaped at the basement door standing wide open. With the alarm screaming in her ears, Paige stumbled to the opening, frantically trying to remember the code she'd recently changed when the weird feeling of being watched after Samuel's death had grown stronger. The numbers appeared in her mind, and she quickly tapped the keypad.

Blessed silence followed.

"Before you ask, I must have been on autopilot when I set the alarm." After the itchy sensation of being watched, Paige had been extremely cautious. "The tenants have keys to the basement. One of them must have come down and accidentally set it off." She thought for a moment. "I just remembered that the O'Conners told me they might get some of their things this weekend."

Jason glanced around. "There's no one here."

"Maybe the alarm spooked them," she suggested. "It's not usually on during the day. I shouldn't have set it on a Saturday afternoon."

"Let's go find out."

"I'm sure it's a tenant," Paige insisted.

"Who else would it be?" he asked.

Good question. If Paige told him about her recent concerns of prying eyes and threatening phone calls, would he think she'd made it all up?

After being on high alert, Paige wasn't thrilled about going down into the dreary confines of the basement, but it was her job to find out what had happened. She told herself that there was a simple explanation.

They descended the stairs, Paige taking note of the basement bathed in darkness. It had been cold and uninviting before, but now it was downright ominous. There was no sign of the O'Conners or any other tenants. Whoever had gone in hadn't bothered with the lights.

Once they reached the bottom of the stairs, Paige followed Jason farther into the space. The air was so thick it seemed to clog her lungs, and she could swear she heard scratching sounds in the corners. Dragging footsteps? She took a deep breath to steady her nerves. What was moving around in the shadows? She clicked on the overhead light.

At the opposite end of the room, rushing footsteps sounded on the stairs. Suddenly the far door opened, and sunlight pierced the murkiness.

"The emergency exit," she whispered, heart pounding.

Jason sprinted to the exit, running up the stairs in pursuit.

Paige anxiously scanned the area while she waited.

He was back in less than a minute. "I didn't see anyone out there."

She shook her head. "It doesn't make sense."

"Let's take a closer look," Jason said.

They walked around, investigating the basement to make sure no else had entered.

When Paige reached Samuel's storage unit, she gasped. The sound echoed off the damp walls.

Jason spun around. "What is it?"

"Samuel's storage unit," she replied. "The doors are wide open."

Jason rushed over to her. "I saw you lock these doors."

With shaky hands, Paige reached out to close the door of the storage unit. The lock hung from the wood. "The closet and the lock are old. This morning I noticed that the lock felt loose. I should have replaced it before."

"You didn't know before this morning." Jason checked the other storage units. "Samuel's is the only one that was tampered with. Why?"

Paige still couldn't think straight. There were too many jumbled thoughts racing in her head. "Perhaps someone knew he stored his belongings down here."

But who would that be? Family? Employees? Tenants? She clasped her hands together. "I can't believe we emptied the unit and brought the boxes upstairs before this happened." Suddenly her heart dropped to her stomach. "My office. I forgot to lock it."

Paige ran upstairs to find the office door still closed. She sprinted inside, her chest aching from exertion. Her keys were on the desk where she'd left them, untouched, along with the four boxes. She sagged against the doorjamb. Samuel's belongings were safe.

Crossing the room, Paige snatched up the keys she'd forgotten and made sure to lock up on the way out. She barely fired on all cylinders lately.

A door opened, and Mrs. Amelia Rice popped her head out. "What was all that racket earlier?"

Paige straightened and focused on her older tenant. "I'm sorry for the noise. I was working in the basement, and the alarm accidentally went off."

Concern crossed Mrs. Rice's face. "Is everything all right?"

"It won't happen again."

Her nonanswer appeared to satisfy Mrs. Rice. The woman nodded and went back inside.

Paige returned to the basement. "The boxes are still in my office."

"That's good." Jason motioned to the far door where the intruder had escaped. "Let's check it out."

She followed him up the stairs.

"This exit isn't used very often, is it?" Jason remarked.

"Since it is an egress, we couldn't close it off permanently, but most people do prefer to use the other door," Paige said. She studied the horizontal panic bar. "This is new."

"What is?"

"This isn't the lock system I remember being installed," she answered. "We had a dead bolt, not a panic bar."

Jason raised his eyebrows. "How could there be a new exit device without you knowing?"

Paige said the first thing that popped into her mind. "Maybe Charlie installed it."

"The handyman?" He frowned. "Did Samuel ask him to add the lock?"

"I'm not sure. From time to time, Charlie takes care of things around the property without telling me. If Samuel asked him, he would have followed through."

"Why would Samuel have asked Charlie to change the setup on this door?"

"I really don't know." She told the truth, but she hated that the admission made her seem incompetent. Ever since Samuel had hired Charlie, he'd taken care of security issues without her asking. He'd been even more diligent since Samuel had died. But could it be a cover for something else?

Paige crossed her arms over her chest. "Samuel didn't like having two doors down here, but he understood it was necessary to comply with the building code."

"He told you that?"

"Yes. But lately . . ." She let her voice trail off. Should she tell him about Samuel's warning before his death?

"Lately?" Jason prompted.

"Samuel had urged me to be more cautious," Paige answered in a clipped tone.

He ran a hand over the back of his neck. "What specifically did he want you to be cautious about?"

"He never actually said. He asked that I keep my eyes open."

Jason pushed against the panic bar. The door opened and closed smoothly. "It's an easy way to get out."

"But not in," she added.

He nodded. "Let's go back and check Samuel's storage unit."

Once there, Paige examined the lock. "I know Charlie never replaced this lock."

Suddenly there was a flash of sunlight as the main door burst open. Footsteps thundered down the staircase.

Jason angled himself in front of Paige, aiming to protect her from the tall, well-built man entering the basement. He had straggly black hair, and Jason guessed that he was in his early thirties.

"Charlie," Paige whispered. Her shoulders sagged. "Over here," she called to the handyman.

Charlie set down a yellow toolbox and walked their way. "Why did the alarm ring? Lexi said you switched it off this morning."

"You talked to Lexi?" Paige asked.

"Yeah, I spoke to her before she ran off somewhere," Charlie explained. "I was heading to Mrs. Nelson's place, but I had to take care of the broken dryer in the laundry room first."

Paige appeared confused, but she quickly shook it off. "I'm glad you made it today."

"Sorry." Charlie stuck his hands into his pockets. "I've been bummed about Samuel."

"I understand, but we need to be on the same page," she said. "You scared the life out of me just now."

"How did I scare you?" Charlie asked.

"Someone broke into the basement," Paige said.

Jason watched Charlie's reaction closely. The man seemed surprised, but it was possible that he was simply a good actor.

"What happened?" Charlie asked.

"I thought the O'Conners might have used their key and accidentally tripped the alarm," Paige said. "But when we got here, no one was waiting for us. Then someone ran up the opposite stairs." She motioned to the emergency exit. "You didn't notice anyone on your way here?"

Charlie shook his head.

Paige frowned at him. "Why are you here?"

"The alarm going off in the middle of the day surprised me." Charlie sounded annoyed at the line of questioning. "You changed the code, so I couldn't disable the alarm. I went to your apartment to find you, but you weren't there."

"We must have missed each other when we came to check out the alarm," Paige said. "As for the code, I haven't seen you lately to give you the new sequence."

Charlie scratched his head. "Why did you set the alarm during the day?"

"We were working, and I didn't even think about what I was doing." Paige shrugged. "Habit, I suppose."

"That doesn't sound like you," Charlie said in an accusatory tone.

Jason wondered why Charlie wasn't cutting Paige any slack. Was the handyman trying to deflect attention from his own actions?

"I don't want to play the blame game," Paige said to Charlie. "But every time I go by the office, you're out or busy, and you've been late for work more days than I can count. Sometimes I can't reach you at all."

Charlie blinked and took a step back, obviously startled. "Okay, yeah, I've been a little sidetracked lately."

"A little?" she repeated.

Charlie's expression turned stony. "Samuel's death hasn't thrown you for a loop too?"

"Of course. Between the funeral and other things . . ." Paige swallowed. "It's going to take us both a while to come to terms with his passing."

Charlie regarded Jason as if he suddenly noticed him. "You're the new tenant," he said, suspicion etching his face.

Jason crossed his arms over his chest. "That's right."

"I saw you the day you came to sign the lease," Charlie continued. "What are you doing down here?"

"Paige and I were talking when the alarm went off," Jason explained. "I didn't want her to check out the basement alone."

"Are you sure it was an intruder?" Charlie asked Paige.

"I think it's the most likely explanation, but whoever it was took off before we saw them." Paige paused. "Why did you change the lock on the emergency exit door?"

"It was time for an upgrade," Charlie replied.

"At Samuel's request?" Paige persisted.

Charlie shuffled his feet. "Yeah."

Jason didn't miss the guilt that flashed in Charlie's eyes. The handyman was routinely late for work, sometimes Paige couldn't contact him, and he and Samuel kept secrets. What else was Charlie hiding from Paige?

"Well, I wasn't informed of that, so it was a bit of a surprise," Paige said. "What was even more surprising was the storage closet."

"What are you talking about?" Charlie asked.

"Samuel's personal storage closet was wide open," Paige answered.

"No way," Charlie said as he rushed over to the unit.

Jason and Paige joined him.

"Where are all his things?" Charlie asked, gaping at the empty storage closet.

"We boxed them up and carried them to the office this morning," Paige said.

Charlie scowled at her. "I didn't know you were cleaning it out so soon."

"I thought I should honor his request right away," Paige said softly.

Charlie gestured to the open doors. "And you closed it up?"

She nodded.

"I saw her do it," Jason confirmed.

"I'm confused." Creases formed between Charlie's bushy eyebrows. "So who was down here?"

"That's the question of the day," Jason muttered.

Charlie clenched his fists. "This doesn't make sense."

"None of it does," Paige said.

"You think someone who doesn't live here opened the door and triggered the alarm?" Charlie asked, clearly trying to understand what had happened. "The alarm spooked whoever it was, and they took off?"

"Why else would they run away instead of waiting to tell us they set off the alarm?" Paige asked, her voice rising.

"But why enter the basement with the alarm blaring?" Charlie asked. "The person had to know that they were likely to get caught."

"Another stellar question," Jason said.

"Are you going to call the police?" Charlie asked.

Paige hesitated as she appeared to mull over the question.

Jason felt his chest tighten at her indecision. He wished he could do something to help her, but he had no idea what.

A beep sounded, and Charlie pulled his phone from his belt. "It's Mrs. Nelson. She's waiting for me."

"Go ahead," Paige said. "We'll figure everything out later."

"I'm sorry," Charlie said. "I didn't mean to upset you."

"It's been a long and emotional week," Paige said. "Stop by the office later, and I'll give you the new code."

"Lock up after me," Charlie instructed. He glared at Jason, then retrieved his toolbox and headed to the emergency exit as if to check it out himself.

As Charlie climbed the stairs, a ringtone sounded, followed by Charlie answering his phone. His voice faded as he opened the door and moved outside.

Jason turned to Paige. "Want to fill me in?"

She raised her eyebrows. "On what?"

"'Between the funeral and other things . . .'" He let his voice trail off as she had done earlier.

"You noticed that?"

"I told you," Jason said. "I like to figure things out."

Paige sighed. "After Lexi came home from school yesterday, we had an argument." She waved her hand dismissively. "That's not important. But she went out to the courtyard to read. I stood in my doorway, wondering where my little girl went."

"Was it that bad of a disagreement?"

"I don't like being at odds with my daughter," she replied.

He didn't have kids, but he couldn't miss the devotion in Paige's voice whenever she mentioned Lexi.

"Anyway, I felt someone watching me."

"Who?" Jason asked, feeling his composure start to slip.

"I don't know," Paige said. "I checked around and didn't see anything out of the ordinary. But the sensation wouldn't go away. It was like a tingling at the back of my neck."

"So you're thinking that if someone was watching you, they could have tried to get into the basement?"

"Yes, and I don't want Charlie to know," she admitted. "He hasn't been reliable lately, and ever since the funeral, it's been weird."

"I get it." He took her elbow and steered her toward the storage closet. "This, however, could have been someone specifically tampering with the lock."

"Or it's an old lock that finally broke loose," Paige reasoned.

"I suppose it's too much to ask if there are security cameras down here."

"As I already mentioned, Samuel was a little slow catching up to technology," she replied. "Plus, we've never had any problems since I started working here. Should we call the police?"

"And tell them what?" Jason asked. "That there was a mix-up? An intruder might have been here, but neither of us saw them? That the lock malfunctioned?"

"When you put it that way, it does sound ridiculous." Paige tapped her chin with her finger. "Do you think Charlie had anything to do with it?"

"You know him better than I do, but I doubt it." He had reservations about Charlie, but his gut reaction told him that the handyman hadn't been behind this.

"Why not?"

"Charlie could get the alarm code from you and come down anytime he wanted without you knowing," Jason reminded her. "Also, Samuel asked him to install the bar on the door. No, Charlie wasn't involved. At least, not that way."

She rubbed her hands up and down her arms. "But someone was."

"We're all on guard now," he said, trying to make her feel better. "Charlie will most likely be more vigilant too."

Paige nodded.

"What do you say we lock up and get out of here?" Jason suggested. "You probably need some time to clear your head."

"That's a good idea," she said. "Walking to the marina always gives me clarity."

He smiled. "Then we'll take a walk."

At the top of the stairs, Paige went to set the alarm again, then stopped herself. Shaking her head, she pulled her keys from her pocket, then pressed the fob to lock the door.

Now that the excitement had passed, Jason allowed himself to consider the situation. Multiple scenarios ran through his mind. This could have been a robbery gone wrong, a freaked-out tenant, or an old piece of wood not holding the original lock in the storage unit. But remembering the intruder's footsteps on the stairs ratcheted up his need to take Paige's safety seriously. Still, he didn't want her to live in fear.

"Listen, this might not have been a coincidence," he told her as they headed to their apartments.

"It might have been that my mind is elsewhere, and I messed up," she said. "Since I got the news of Samuel's death, I've been in a fog. Even Lexi has been accusing me of being forgetful."

"It's hard to grieve a loved one," Jason said, "but you need to focus."

"I know. And I will."

As they reached their apartments, he noticed Lexi pacing in the courtyard, talking on her phone and smiling.

Paige waved to get her daughter's attention.

When Lexi saw them, her expression abruptly changed. She spoke a few words into the phone and hung up.

"If you don't mind, I'm going to stay home with my daughter," Paige said to Jason. "Maybe we can walk to the marina some other time."

"Sure." He reached out and squeezed her arm. "I'm only a door away. Let me know if you need anything."

"Thanks." She smiled at her daughter as Lexi approached them. "Who were you talking to?"

"No one," Lexi said, then glanced at Jason.

He recognized the challenge in the teenager's eyes. Paige hadn't witnessed Lexi's actions in the basement when they were packing Samuel's belongings, but he had. Was Lexi a thief? Jason sincerely hoped not. But until they had a chance to discuss it, he decided to keep his suspicions to himself.

As Paige and Lexi walked away and disappeared into their apartment, Jason studied the building. He didn't like how today's events had gone down. Not one little bit.

Now he had more questions to throw into the mix. Who had Lexi been talking to? And why didn't she want to tell her mother?

After another restless night, Paige woke up with a mild headache. Images of shadowy figures running up the basement stairs had invaded her dreams. She shivered at the notion. She and Jason had narrowly missed a close encounter with an intruder yesterday.

After Paige got out of bed, she ran into a quiet Lexi in the hallway outside the bathroom.

"I don't feel like cooking this morning," Paige said. "What do you think about going out for breakfast?"

"Okay," Lexi said.

It wasn't an enthusiastic response, but Paige was glad that she'd at least agreed. Maybe they'd be able to have a good talk over the meal.

They both dressed in T-shirts and shorts, then walked the two blocks to their favorite restaurant for French toast and a positive conversation. But as usual, they argued over the part-time job that Lexi wanted. Paige reflected that getting one of the two things she'd hoped for wasn't so bad.

On their way back home, they bumped into Jason. Their neighbor was out for a run and dressed in athletic gear.

"Good morning," he called out, stopping when he reached them.

Paige smiled, glad to see him despite everything that was going on. The attraction she'd noticed when they first met seemed to grow with the time they spent together. She hadn't been searching for any kind of relationship, but she couldn't deny her interest in getting to know him better.

Clearly bored, Lexi announced, "I'm going home."

Paige felt torn. She wanted to make some strides with Lexi, but she recognized the stubborn set of her daughter's mouth. "Go ahead."

Lexi strode away, already tapping on her phone.

"Is everything okay?" Jason asked.

"Tough morning." Paige let out a sigh. "We had the same argument about Lexi getting a job, which led to her conversation with Charlie."

"About the alarm?"

She nodded. "She asked who cared that she'd told Charlie about the alarm. I didn't make a big deal about it."

"Do you think she went back to the basement to get something and got spooked when the alarm went off?"

"She would have told me," Paige said defensively. But the flash of guilt on Lexi's face when Paige had asked her what she'd been up to had made Paige suspicious.

"I'm sorry," he said. "I didn't mean to imply that Lexi was the intruder."

"After the shock of Samuel's passing, I've probably made too big a deal out of everything that's happened the past couple of days. Especially with Lexi." She grimaced. "I hope you don't think I'm losing it."

"No, but you shouldn't ignore your gut reaction," Jason advised. "It's there for a reason."

"Do you believe I'm making things more complicated than they are?" Paige asked.

"I can't answer that," he said. "Maybe having a sit-down with Lexi to clear the air would help you both."

"Lexi has been acting unusual lately," she admitted. "She must be reacting to my crazy moods."

"You should talk to her," Jason insisted.

Paige realized she was backpedaling, but she wondered why he was so adamant about her having a conversation with Lexi. Deciding a change of subject was in order, Paige asked, "Did you just start your run?"

"Yeah, I'm going to swing by the beach," he replied. His expression softened. "But I'm in no hurry. I can hang out if you want some company."

"Don't let me keep you," she said, touched by his kind offer. "Besides, I have a few things to do around the building anyway."

"I thought you didn't work on Sundays," Jason said with a teasing smile, which made him even more handsome.

"You remember that?"

"I remember everything."

Paige had to suppress a pleasant shiver over his easily spoken words. "I try not to work on Sundays, but I got behind because of the funeral and then yesterday's events. No days off for a busy manager."

"Then you should get to it," he said.

She wanted to linger and continue talking to this compelling man, but her duties awaited. "I'll see you later."

Jason hesitated, then resumed his run.

Paige watched him go, enjoying the controlled pace and the way his broad shoulders moved with ease, and then she mustered up the energy to get to work.

As Paige neared the apartment building, she realized the odd sense of being watched didn't follow her today, but that didn't mean she'd dismissed the inner warning. The prickly awareness of late had her on edge, but after the near miss with an intruder in the basement? It now fell into a completely different category.

She went straight to the office to retrieve her clipboard, reading over a list of work orders she needed to confirm. A light bulb was out on the third floor near Mrs. Nelson's door. The second-floor banister was loose. She decided to head up to the top floor first, then work her way down.

As Paige climbed the steps, she continued reading her list. Voices sounded above her, one male and one female. Some of the tenants visiting? She grinned as she grew closer. Maybe catching up with the people who lived here would take her mind off her suddenly tumultuous life for a while.

A meow came out of nowhere, and Gus trotted up to her. When he rubbed against her leg, her stress level immediately dipped. She took comfort in his calming presence.

"It's good to see you." Paige bent down to rub his fur. His loud purring brought a smile to her lips. Once he'd had enough attention, she continued on her way, cat in tow.

She chuckled, imagining Gus as her protector while she made her rounds.

When Paige reached the bend to head up to the second floor, she froze as a man rushed down. It took a moment to recognize Samuel's nephew, Bennett Calhoun. She'd never seen him on the property before.

Bennett appeared disheveled. His hair fell over his forehead, and his ill-fitting suit had seen better days. The buttons of the jacket strained against the bulk of his midsection, and the hems of his pants were worn and frayed.

Bennett stared at her in surprise. Then he smiled, but it didn't quite reach his eyes. "I was hoping to run into you."

Her defenses were up in a flash. "Can I help you with something?"

"I came to walk the property," he replied.

Paige blinked. "Why?"

Bennett straightened his shoulders. "You are aware that I might be your boss in the near future, aren't you?"

Did he know something she didn't? "I didn't realize the conditions of Samuel's will had been released."

"That's just a formality." He glanced around. "Let's talk in your office."

"Certainly." Paige led the way.

Gus trotted at her side, his tail in the air.

"Whose animal is that?" Bennett asked.

She stopped and turned to find him scowling down at Gus. "Everyone's."

Bennett waved a hand as if to shoo Gus away. "He needs to go."

Paige pressed her lips together, remaining silent. She refused to pick a fight with this unpleasant man or get rid of the cat the tenants adored.

As if sensing danger, Gus ran down the stairs and disappeared.

The fissure of awareness that had tickled the back of her neck on Friday returned. She rolled her shoulders to get rid of the sensation, but it remained.

They arrived at the office, and Paige unlocked the door.

Once inside, Bennett strode across the room and sat down behind her desk as if he came to work here every day.

Unsure what to do, she stood by the door, hugging the clipboard to her chest.

"I want to see your financial reports," he said.

"I can't do that."

Irritation flashed across his face. "Why not?"

"Because legally, you don't own the property yet."

Bennett waved a hand dismissively. "It's only a formality."

Paige stood her ground, even as her knees quaked. "I'm sorry, but I can't help you."

"You can't?" He rested his elbows on the desk and narrowed his eyes. "Or you won't?"

"Legally, I can't. Not until the will is read and Samuel's wishes are revealed."

"You'd better watch out," Bennett warned. "You're putting your job on the line."

She didn't know how to respond. After Mason's phone call, she'd been worried that she might be unemployed again. Taking a stand right now might not be wise for her future, but she wouldn't cross the line. She owed Samuel that much.

He leaned back, the seams of his jacket straining, and regarded her. "Samuel didn't fill you in on his secrets, did he?"

"Excuse me?"

"He had plenty of secrets."

Paige wondered if this was why Samuel had sounded so concerned in the last message he left her. Had Bennett been bothering him, and Samuel had wanted to warn Paige about him?

"What did he tell you about our family?" Bennett asked.

"Not much," she hedged.

"Figures," he muttered.

"Please—"

"Don't interrupt me," Bennett said. "My mother should have owned this property. She was the oldest. The first in line. Samuel intentionally kept it from her. Selfish man."

Paige wanted to protest, because that didn't sound like the Samuel she knew, but she remained silent.

"He made sure we were left out of our ancestor's final wishes," he continued, bitterness radiating from him in waves. "Samuel stole my legacy."

"I think—"

Bennett held up his hand, cutting her off. "Let me finish." He leaned forward again. "Before my mother died, she told my father that there were papers proving she should have been the sole owner of this building before Samuel swooped in behind her back and bought the property."

Paige was surprised. She'd never heard anything about that. "Do you have those papers?"

His expression turned to steel. "I have people looking into them."

So he didn't have the documents. Was he searching for them here? Could that explain the intruder in the basement? Her insides started shaking at the idea.

"They were lost over the years." Bennett waved his hand as if dismissing a small detail that didn't matter. "My great-grandfather and a partner bought this property prior to World War II. Together they drew up plans for this building. He made it known to the family that he wanted my mother, not Samuel, to have control."

Paige recalled the information she'd garnered on the history of Poinciana Arms when she'd started working here. The older but well-maintained buildings dotting downtown were being torn down, and Samuel had been concerned about their rich histories being lost forever. As Paige had researched a way to keep the historical places intact, she'd learned that the property Poinciana Arms sat on was the land the men had purchased like Bennett said, but the construction of the apartment building hadn't begun until the early 1950s.

The problem with Bennett's claim was that his great-grandfather had died before returning from the war. His partner eventually constructed the building, but he sold the property to a young Samuel, who had taken over the barely occupied building and transformed it into a moneymaking enterprise.

"Samuel never mentioned a problem with ownership," Paige remarked.

"He wouldn't," Bennett said, his tone tinged with animosity. "The smug man always assumed he was right."

"But you don't have any proof," she reminded him.

"Not yet. But I will." He rose, then slapped his palms on the desk. "My mother always said we should have owned this property and gotten the revenue that came with it."

Paige tried to remain calm even as her anxiety increased. "Did your mother ever try to dispute Samuel's legal claim?"

"Samuel always told her the original deal had changed." Bennett shook his head. "He broke her spirit in the process."

"This sounds like a family issue," she responded. "Maybe a lawyer should be involved."

"Don't worry. I'm planning to hire an attorney."

Paige didn't like the sound of that, but she wasn't prepared to hear any more details. She changed the subject. "I still don't understand why you're here today."

"I'm checking over my property," he said. "Making sure it's in shipshape before I take over."

"Samuel never let this building fall into disrepair," she said, defending her mentor and friend. "We've always maintained and updated the property so the tenants have a safe place to live."

Bennett huffed. "So you say."

"Samuel took great pride in Poinciana Arms," Paige said. "We worked together to—"

"You and Samuel may have been close, but don't expect me to keep you on staff."

She flinched at the threat. Lexi's angry face flashed in her mind. They were growing apart. If Paige lost her job, would she also lose her daughter in a custody battle too? She tried to control her panic. "Until the will is read, there's nothing I can do."

"No matter. We'll know soon enough." He rounded the desk, stopping before her. "In the meantime, I'm going to continue my walk around the property."

Locking her knees to keep them from buckling, she said with an authority she didn't feel, "I'm afraid I must ask you to leave."

Bennett raised an eyebrow. "Are you serious?"

"Technically you're trespassing," Paige said. "You don't live here, and you don't own the property, so there's no reason for you to be roaming around uninvited."

His expression suddenly became menacing. "And you think you can stop me?"

It took everything in her to stand her ground. "If you don't leave right now, I will call the police."

"Who cares? They won't do anything."

"I guess we'll find out when they get here," Paige said as she removed her phone from her pocket.

Bennett pointed at her. "You're not helping yourself."

"Maybe not," she admitted. "But I'm the manager until told otherwise by legal authorities."

He backed up, his cheeks reddening. "This is not the end of the discussion."

Paige swallowed hard. "Today it is."

Bennett glared at her, then stalked out of the office.

When he was gone, she sagged against the door, leaned her head back against it, and steadied her breathing.

If Paige thought the unsettling events going on around her were random, had Bennett Calhoun's appearance proven otherwise?

Jason slowed as he walked up the sidewalk toward his apartment, examining the small shell he'd found. He planned to give it to Paige.

A man wearing a suit stormed past, banging into Jason's shoulder. "Get out of my way," the man barked.

Jason watched the stranger rush down the street and climb into a run-down sedan. The car chugged as it started, emitting a loud noise and a puff of smoke, then zipped down the street and out of sight.

"What was that all about?" Jason muttered. He slipped the shell into his pocket and resumed his walk. As he passed the office, he noticed Paige leaning against the door, her hand pressed against her chest. "Are you okay?" he asked.

She flinched at his voice. Recognizing him, she straightened her shoulders and smiled. "Oh, you're back."

He noticed the shadows lingering in her expression. "Are you still having a bad day?"

Paige stared down at her clipboard. "You could say that."

"Then this should brighten your mood." Jason smiled. "Close your eyes, and hold out your hand."

She did as he asked. "I'm intrigued," she said, humor lacing her tone.

He took the shell out of his pocket and dropped it into her palm. "Okay, take a peek."

Paige obeyed. "It's a star."

"Not exactly."

"Okay, a shell in the general shape of a star," Paige amended. She studied the shell more closely. "It's chipped."

"Yeah, that's what gives it the star shape," Jason said.

She blinked at him in surprise. "You remembered."

"You and Lexi seemed so taken by Samuel's stories about the constellations. When I ran over the shell, it made me think of Samuel and his daughter's interest in astronomy."

Her laughter floated in the air. "How did you run over it?"

"It was because of a football."

"I'm going to need more information than that."

"I was running down the beach, minding my own business. Suddenly out of the blue, a projectile headed in my direction. I dropped to my knees, waiting for the coast to clear. When the kids playing catch gave me the thumbs-up, I put my hands on the sand to push off, and the shell dug into my palm. I investigated, and this is what I found."

"That's quite a story," Paige commented, but the corners of her lips twitched in a grin.

"What can I say?" he asked. "I like to keep things interesting."

"Thank you." She gazed down at the shell nestled in her hand. "I'll keep it on my desk where I'll see it every day."

In the short time Jason had known Paige, she'd somehow become even prettier. Yes, she had definitely managed to get under his skin.

Paige cupped her hands together, protecting the shell. "And in case you're wondering, you made my day."

His mood elevated even more at her admission. "My intention all along."

She smiled.

"Are you done for the day?" Jason asked, hoping she might want to hang out with him.

"I wish, especially since I just had the strangest run-in."

He frowned. "Another one?"

"Believe it or not, yes."

"I go for a run and come back to find you knee-deep in drama," Jason teased.

Paige laughed. "I feel like that's my life lately." Shaking her head, she moved inside the office, then set her clipboard and the shell on the desk. "Samuel's nephew, Bennett Calhoun, paid me a surprise visit."

He followed her into the office and jerked his thumb over his shoulder. "Guy in a suit? I think I passed him out front."

"He took off when I wouldn't give him access to the property."

"This property?" Jason asked. "Why?"

"Bennett's under the impression he owns Poinciana Arms," she answered. "It sounds like some kind of old family feud."

"He told you that?"

"Yes. Bennett's planning on taking over once the will is read."

"Did Samuel ever tell you what his plans were if anything happened to him?"

"No, he never said." She cleared her throat, blinking rapidly. "Why would he? I don't know if he even had a plan. I'm sure he never imagined he'd be taken away in a car accident."

He leaned his hip against the desk. "I thought I'd moved into a quiet building when I signed the lease."

"Normally it is," Paige said.

"No one would blame you if you took a few days off," Jason told her gently.

"I can't. Especially not with Bennett nosing around." She stared across the room as if trying to decide whether to tell him something. Finally, she said, "Bennett mentioned some papers that would prove he's the rightful owner."

"Did he show them to you?"

"No, it doesn't sound like he has them." Paige frowned, apparently mulling over the situation. "Do you think Bennett could have been hiding out and watching me? Maybe he thinks the papers are here, and he's trying to find them."

"Did he say they were on the premises?" he asked.

"All he said is that people are looking into them." She paused. "You didn't see Bennett's expression. This is not a man who is going to give up until he gets what he wants."

"It all comes down to proof."

"I don't think he knows much more than what he's heard over the years," Paige said. "He and Samuel never had a close relationship."

"But he could be telling the truth?"

Pain dulled her eyes. "Samuel told me a little about his family history, but obviously there is something going on that he never mentioned."

Jason searched her face. "Are you worried about Bennett?"

Paige swayed slightly. "Not really."

"That's not very convincing."

"He can't legally do anything to affect me right now. Like I told him, until the will is read, I'm still the manager." She raised her chin. "And I'm not going to let his threats put me on edge."

Jason admired her courage, but he wondered how far Bennett would go to get what he wanted. He was afraid that Paige might be in danger. "Do you have anything to protect yourself? Like pepper spray?"

Paige blew out a breath. "Well, if I wasn't worried before, I am now."

"I'm serious," he said. "You should be prepared."

"I'll think about it." She picked up her clipboard. "Now I'd better get back to work."

"I'm sorry," Jason said. "I didn't mean to frighten you."

"It's okay. I appreciate your concern." Her lips curved into a small smile. "Thanks for listening. It's nice to have someone to talk to."

"I'm here if you need me. You know that, right?"

"I do, but this is probably all a big mistake," Paige said. "Everything's going to be fine. There's nothing to be worried about."

Jason wondered if she was trying to convince him—or herself.

Paige had almost no time to brood over what Bennett was up to on Monday. Work kept her hopping all day, fielding phone calls from tenants, finishing paperwork, and running several errands.

Late that afternoon when she was going through the mail, her attention wavered as she glimpsed the shell Jason had given her. She smiled as she picked it up, running a finger along the rough edges.

A funny sensation gripped her heart. She couldn't recall a time when a guy had discovered a token this delicate and thought to give it to her. Plus, Jason had remembered her telling him about Samuel's love for the stars. He listened. It was rare for her to feel heard when she'd lived in the shadow of her parents' and Kevin's careers. In that way, Jason and Samuel were a lot alike. She wished they had been able to meet. The two men would have gotten along well.

Paige tried not to read anything into the gesture, but it was hard to ignore Jason. And honestly, she didn't want to. She propped the shell against the pen holder.

Charlie lumbered into the office, making her jump. It seemed she automatically went on high alert these days, especially after yesterday's confrontation with Bennett.

"How's it going?" he asked, setting his yellow toolbox on his desk. Today he'd pulled his straggly hair into a loose ponytail.

She took a calming breath. "I'm about ready to close up for the day. You?"

Charlie dropped into one of the chairs in front of her desk. "I finally finished up at Mrs. Nelson's place."

"Good," Paige said. "She must be relieved."

"She is. But that woman does love to talk."

She recognized the fondness in his tone. Everyone had a soft spot for Mrs. Nelson. "I imagine that comes from living alone."

"She's insisting that someone came into her apartment uninvited," Charlie said, "even though I told her no one else has permission to be in there other than me, and I'd never do it without her knowledge."

Surprised, Paige asked, "She mentioned that?"

"Yep." He crossed one leg over the other. "She told you too?"

"Yes. I tried to reassure her, but I guess she didn't believe me."

"It's probably my fault anyway," Charlie said with a sigh.

Paige tilted her head. "Why would it be your fault?"

"I've been in and out of her place since I started the project," he explained. "Muffin was usually in my way while I worked, so I was constantly chasing her off. I probably knocked over one of her collectibles and didn't realize it."

Relief washed through Paige. After Bennett's visit, she'd wondered if he'd taken to lurking in the shadows before breaking into apartments. She chided herself for the ridiculous thought and debated mentioning Bennett's visit to Charlie. No, she wouldn't tell him until she knew more about Bennett's intentions. Why worry him over nothing?

Charlie chuckled. "She even told Lexi about her suspicions."

"Really?" Her daughter hadn't mentioned that conversation. She'd also denied setting the alarm off on Saturday and sworn she hadn't returned to the basement.

The topic of conversation lately revolved around the merits of her getting a summer job, which either turned into an argument or steely silence. As Paige repeatedly told Lexi, babysitting Muffin and doing odd errands around the property might not be what she considered fun, but it brought in spending money. Paige knew that what Lexi considered fun consisted of visiting her father for two weeks every summer. She had to hope her daughter or Kevin didn't want to change the current custody arrangements because Lexi didn't get her way.

Paige's worries grew by the day.

A sheepish look passed over Charlie's face. "Hey, listen. I wanted to apologize about getting our wires crossed on Saturday."

"You'll have to be more specific," she said with what she hoped came off as humor. "I had a crazy day."

"I'm sorry about not telling you that I'd installed the panic bar on the emergency exit door in the basement," he clarified. "Samuel asked me to take care of it, and after he died, I forgot about it. I didn't mean to upset you."

"It's all right," Paige assured him. "It came as a surprise, but I'm up to speed now."

"It seemed like more," Charlie said. "Are you mad at me?"

She wasn't mad, but she was still concerned by his recent actions. And why was he using a placating tone now after he'd been short with her lately? "No, but I think going forward, we need to have better communication."

"Agreed, since it's only the two of us now."

A wave of sadness settled over her as a thick grief blanketed the room. Paige shook it off and grabbed a sticky note. She jotted down the new code sequence for the basement alarm, peeled the note off the pad, and handed it across the desk to Charlie. "Here's the new alarm code."

"Thanks." He tucked it into his shirt pocket. "So what's up with the new tenant?"

"Jason Bronson?"

"Yeah, you guys were pretty cozy when I saw you in the basement."

Paige sat back in her chair. Why was Charlie questioning her about Jason? Then she realized what Charlie had said, that it was only the two of them now. Could his concern be more than as a coworker? Her gaze flitted to Jason's shell. "He offered to help Lexi and me empty Samuel's storage unit—that's all. I thought it would be a good way to introduce him to life at Poinciana Arms."

Charlie furrowed his brow. "By going through Samuel's stuff?"

"We were very respectful." She pointed to the four boxes under the window. "They're safe here."

Charlie glanced over his shoulder. When he turned back around, his eyes were filled with skepticism. "Be careful."

His sudden concern rankled her. "Why would you warn me about Jason?"

"You don't really know him," he said. "He's basically a stranger."

"What's with the big-brother act?" Paige asked.

"I think Samuel would want me to watch out for you and Lexi."

"Thanks, but we're fine." She folded her hands on top of the desk.

"Even though you think someone broke into the basement?" Charlie asked.

"I'm being careful," Paige said. "How about you?"

He raised his eyebrows. "What do you mean?"

"Since the news about Samuel and the funeral."

"I'm processing." Charlie paused. "You didn't call me on Sunday, so I had a quiet day."

She felt guilty not telling him about Bennett's visit, but she stuck to her original decision to wait for the right time to mention it. They had more important matters to discuss. "Since we're clearing the air, I have to ask you something. Why have you been showing up late for work and not answering my calls? Is there something I need to know?"

"I think Samuel's passing got to me," he responded quietly.

Paige understood Charlie's grief, but this trend had started before Samuel died. "Is it going to be an ongoing problem?"

"Nah." Charlie suddenly stood up. "I know what my job here entails." He collected his toolbox and walked out the door.

"That went well," she muttered to the empty room.

As Paige tidied her desk, she ran a gentle finger over the star-shaped shell. She'd known Jason for a few days, but it felt like they were longtime friends. Was it okay to start having feelings for him, especially when she hadn't been exploring the possibilities? The hope of a relationship at this point in her life had been more of a dream than reality, but Paige didn't want to be alone forever.

She shut down the computer when she noticed Lexi walk by the window. Paige called out her daughter's name, but she didn't get an answer.

After collecting her things and locking the office, Paige let herself into the apartment.

Lexi stood in the kitchen on her phone. When she noticed Paige, her eyes went wide. "I have to go," she mumbled into the phone, then disconnected the call.

"You're late getting home from school," Paige commented from the counter separating the living room from the kitchen. She felt as if she were walking on eggshells. These days, she had to be a mind reader to figure out Lexi's moods.

Lexi slipped her phone into her back pocket. "I was hanging out with friends."

"On the school campus?" Paige asked.

Lexi opened the refrigerator door and peered inside. "No, we were at the park, catching up."

"You don't see them enough during classes?" Paige asked.

"We're not together all day," Lexi said in a tone that implied Paige couldn't possibly remember her high school days. "We take different subjects, and it's not like we can talk during the classes we do have together."

Paige decided to change the subject before her daughter shut down. "So, is there anything new?"

Lexi shut the fridge and turned around, a can of soda in her hand. "What's with all the questions?"

Paige shrugged. "I was wondering if you went back to Mrs. Kelly's store about the job."

"You made it pretty clear you don't want me to work there."

Paige had been mulling over the job, and she'd decided that it might fulfill her daughter and improve her outlook. "Maybe I was wrong."

"Is this a joke?"

"No. You've always been consistent watching Muffin for Mrs. Nelson. Besides, you're right. I can't offer you many fun jobs around here."

"You're serious?" Lexi asked, setting the soda can on the counter.

"Yes, I am," Paige said. "This could be a great experience for you."

"Thank you." Lexi rushed around the counter and hugged Paige. "I won't work too much, and I'll still help around here."

Paige laughed but savored the hug. When Lexi pulled back, with joy bright on her face, a deep sense of happiness infused Paige.

"I'm sure we can work your summer vacation schedule with your dad around a part-time job."

Lexi jumped up and down, then suddenly stopped, frowned, and went back behind the counter. "You won't be sorry."

Paige ignored her daughter's odd reaction, not wanting to ruin the positive mood. "When school starts in the fall, we'll see what's going on and decide if you can work during the school year. Your grades will still come first, of course, but if you like the job and can do both, that can probably be arranged."

Lexi huffed out a breath. "That's a long way off."

"You know me. I'm always planning ahead."

"As long as I don't have to go into that basement again," Lexi said, "I'll take what I can get."

"In the meantime, we'll have to tell your dad about the possible job," Paige said.

"No problem. I talk to him all the time." Lexi lifted her backpack from the counter. "I've got homework. And a job application to fill out." She passed by in a rush.

Paige glanced at the can on the counter. "You forgot your soda."

"I'll drink it later."

"Wait a minute," Paige said.

Lexi stopped. She dropped her backpack on her feet, then reached out for the can.

Paige snatched the can and took a few steps forward to hand it over. "What is wrong with you?" She bent down to pick up the backpack and noticed a pair of pristine pink-and-white sneakers she didn't recognize. "Did you get new shoes?"

"I have money from watching Muffin," Lexi said, dodging the question. She grabbed her backpack and hurried to her room, shutting the door behind her.

Paige stared at the closed door, the barrier between them, and considered her daughter's shoes. Paige had seen enough advertisements to recognize the brand design on the side of the sneaker. She went to her computer, found the brand's website, and almost choked when she read the price. They cost more than a hundred dollars. Lexi hadn't been watching Muffin that much. Where had she gotten the money? Had she been saving up for a long time? Or should Paige be concerned?

Someone knocked on the door.

Paige blew out a breath and opened it to find Aaron Nichols, a thirtysomething tenant from the second floor.

"Good afternoon," Paige said with a smile. "How can I help you?"

"Sorry to bother you, but I have a refrigerator issue."

"I'm sorry about that. Hold on a second, and I'll go with you to check it out." Paige walked to her daughter's room and knocked. "I need to go upstairs. I'll be back soon."

"Okay," came the muffled reply.

Paige took the work order book she kept in the apartment for requests outside of office hours and stepped outside with Aaron.

As they headed toward the stairs, she asked, "So, what's wrong with the fridge?"

"I'm not sure," he said. "Sometimes it doesn't feel as cold as it should, but the food is all right. Then other times it seems to be working normally."

"When did you notice the problem?"

"A few days ago."

When they reached his apartment on the second floor, Aaron unlocked the door.

Paige noticed gouge marks on the outer surface, surrounding the lock. "What's all this?"

"All what?" he asked.

She rested a finger on the scarred wood. "These marks on the door."

"I have no idea." Aaron studied the door. "To be honest, I never noticed them before."

Paige wondered how he could have missed them. Moving in closer, she saw there were three deep lines, surrounded by fainter scratches. "Something happened here."

"It could have been the kids," he suggested, his cheeks reddening.

Aaron and his wife had two young boys. They were rambunctious but sweet. More than once Paige had filled out a work order to have something fixed or replaced in their apartment because of the children.

But after Bennett's surprise visit yesterday, the timing was much too coincidental, especially when he made it clear he was after those papers. Would he be desperate enough to try to break into the tenants' apartments?

"The boys were in and out all day yesterday, playing with their new plastic cars," Aaron explained.

Paige nodded, even though she doubted the marks had been made by children's toys. "Are Abby and the boys home?"

"No, they're visiting Abby's parents." He opened the door and led her into the kitchen.

Paige stood in front of the fridge. Nothing more than a weak hum, but when she opened the door, it did indeed feel warm inside. The internal thermostat read higher than it should normally run. "There's definitely a problem."

"Do you think you can get it fixed today?" Aaron asked.

"Hold on." She pulled her phone from the back pocket of her jeans and dialed Charlie.

He answered on the second ring. "What's up?"

"Aaron on the second floor has a refrigerator problem," Paige replied. "Are you still on the grounds?"

"Yep. Be there in a few minutes."

She ended the call and told Aaron, "Charlie can give you a better timeline."

"Thanks. Abby wanted me to tell you sooner, but I forgot." He gave a rueful smile. "She wasn't too happy with me."

Paige laughed. "No, I imagine she wasn't."

"I was going to tell you yesterday, but I bumped into a guy on the way to the office. He started asking questions, and I ran out of time."

A whisper of the unease she'd lived with the past few days crept over her. "Who was the guy?"

"I don't know," Aaron said. "I never saw him before, but I think he wants to rent here. He asked a bunch of questions about the place."

Her unease grew. "What kind of questions?"

He sent her a startled glance.

Paige didn't want to worry Aaron with her suspicions, so she quickly came up with an explanation. "No one ever came to inquire about a vacancy, so I'm curious."

"He asked if the rent was affordable." Aaron leaned against the counter. "And if the apartments had been upgraded over the years."

"Perhaps he'll come back," she said, hoping she sounded nonchalant when she had a good idea of who had been asking her tenant about the building. "Could you describe him so I recognize him if he stops by the office?"

"He was in his forties. Brown hair. He wore a suit that must have been awfully stuffy for such a hot day."

Now Paige was certain that Aaron had talked to Bennett. She couldn't believe the nerve of the man.

"This morning I ran into Charlie," he remarked. "I told him about the man."

Paige couldn't believe that Charlie hadn't said a word earlier. Why would he not tell her about Samuel's nephew nosing around the property? But she'd done the same to Charlie. She hadn't told him about her run-in with Bennett either. Paige tried not to overreact, but the warning signs in her head screamed about one too many coincidences in a short period of time.

"The kids were with me," Aaron went on, "and I didn't get a chance to mention the fridge."

There was a knock on the door, and Charlie called out, "Can I come in?"

"Sure," Aaron responded. "We're in the kitchen."

Before Charlie joined them, Paige said to Aaron, "If you see that guy around again, will you call me?"

"Sure thing."

Charlie walked in with his toolbox and examined the appliance while Paige wrote up the work order.

"I think this fridge has seen better days," Charlie concluded.

"I'll place an order tomorrow," she said.

"Thanks," Aaron said. "At least I can tell Abby we'll be getting a new refrigerator."

"I'll inform you when we need to get into the apartment," Paige told him before she and Charlie left.

Once they were outside, Paige pointed out the gouges in the door.

"It must be the kids again," Charlie said.

"What were they doing to make such deep scratches?"

He set his toolbox down and moved closer to study the damage. "They were probably playing with their little cars."

She wondered if Charlie had seen the boys playing with their cars yesterday. "I don't think so. The lines are too thin and precise for a piece of plastic."

"What else would it be?" he asked. "A key? A knife?"

Paige found it curious that Charlie was being so specific and argumentative. "I don't know. That's why I asked you."

"Don't worry about it. I'll buff the scratches out and repaint the entire door. It'll look like new." He picked up his toolbox. "Anything else before I take off?"

She wanted to ask why he kept things from her. Why his excuses were wearing thin. Could he be working for Bennett? That would explain his cryptic remark about knowing what his job entailed. The thought chilled her.

In the long run, Samuel's nephew could be a threat to both of them. Unless things weren't what they seemed and Paige was the only one who needed to steer clear of Bennett.

9

Paige hurried down the stairs to her apartment. Charlie's silence about Bennett bothered her more than she wanted to admit. Why was he keeping things from her? She wasn't sure she wanted an answer.

"Good afternoon."

She jumped at the sound of Jason's voice. Smoothing her features, she smiled at him. "Just getting home from work?"

"Yep." He cocked his head. "You?"

Paige held up the book. "Taking care of a work order."

"Does writing work orders usually leave creases in your forehead?"

She shook her head, giving up her pretense. No way could she keep her concerns off her face.

"I've been told I'm a good listener," Jason said. "I'm here if you want to talk."

He was attentive and handsome. Had Paige won some kind of lottery? Really, the timing of meeting this great guy couldn't have been worse. "You can't possibly be interested in what's going on with me."

"You'd be surprised."

Her stomach flipped. Could she trust Jason? He'd offered to be a sounding board, and she desperately needed someone to talk to. "Charlie warned me not to trust you."

"This coming from the guy you work with who keeps all kinds of secrets from you?" Jason asked.

"There is that."

He waited, obviously giving her the option to confide in him or not.

Going with her innate feeling that he was an honorable man, Paige decided to take that risk. “I know it’s close to dinnertime, but do you want something to drink?”

Jason grinned. “If it’s cold, I’m in.”

She opened her door and led him inside, heading straight for the kitchen. “Tea? Soda?”

“Tea sounds great.”

Paige took two glasses from the cabinet. She filled them with tea from a pitcher in the refrigerator and added ice. When she handed a glass to him, their fingers brushed. A spark of excitement danced across her skin. She chided herself. After all, she had more pressing things to think about than the sparks from Jason’s touch.

She gestured toward the living room. “Please make yourself at home.”

Jason took a seat on one end of the couch.

Paige sat at the other end, kicking off her shoes and tucking her legs underneath her. She breathed in the masculine cologne that floated in her direction and found herself taking comfort in it. The scent settled her and gave her the courage to launch right into the conversation. “Do you believe in coincidences?”

“No,” he answered without hesitation.

She appreciated his directness. Somehow it made her feel less adrift.

“And now you’re going to tell me what those coincidences are, right?” Jason coaxed.

Paige set her glass on the coffee table. “You know how Brian thought a repairman had been in his apartment?”

He nodded and took a sip of his tea. “Go on.”

“What worries me is that it’s not an isolated incident. Mrs. Nelson told me a similar story.”

Jason sat up straighter. “No wonder you went pale when Brian brought it up.”

"I told you about the strong sensation of being watched," she reminded him. "Or it's the building being watched. I'm not sure which."

He remained silent, but his expression was grim.

"I've tried to come up with a reason why," Paige continued, "but personally I haven't done anything to warrant all this snooping. Lexi's dad and I have been at odds over custody from time to time since the divorce, but Kevin would never spy on me."

"So you're thinking it's about the property?"

"Yes," she said. "It all started after Samuel died. The police concluded it was a hit-and-run accident. And when I think back to Samuel's warning, I know it has to be connected."

"Maybe you should tell me everything," Jason said.

Since Paige had already opened the dam, she related how much Bennett's visit bothered her, then told him that Charlie knew about Bennett questioning one of their tenants but hadn't mentioned it to her. She described the gouges on the second-floor door and the threatening phone calls that had put her on guard. Now she refused to answer any number she didn't recognize, letting unknown calls go directly to voice mail. She even admitted her confusion about Mason Trembly's phone call regarding a possible sale of the building.

"I was hoping that all you'd tell me is that people don't randomly go into other people's apartments around here." He ran a hand over his hair and sighed. "This is more than I expected."

"What do I do?" Paige grabbed a throw pillow and hugged it against her chest. "I could talk to Samuel if he were still here. He'd know exactly what to say and do. But now?" She sent him an imploring glance. "I'm not incompetent, but this is more than I envisioned when I took the job as apartment manager."

"It's more than anyone would expect," Jason said.

Paige voiced the question she'd been dwelling on since she began to suspect Charlie had known about Bennett's visit and not told her. "Should I call the police?"

He paused as if weighing his answer. "It wouldn't hurt for them to have a report. In case things escalate."

She groaned. "You're right, but I was hoping you wouldn't say that."

He gave her a small, crooked grin. "I'm sorry. What about surveillance around the building?"

"After the eventful weekend, I pulled up the past few days of recordings to check for anything or anyone unusual. But nothing stood out."

"So perhaps someone knew where the cameras were mounted," Jason suggested.

"That's what I'm afraid of," Paige said.

He leaned toward her, his eyes intent and serious. "It couldn't have been random when the alarm went off in the basement."

"I agree. But what could a stranger be after in the basement?"

"Samuel's belongings? His storage unit was wide open."

"Specifically the papers Bennett mentioned." She rubbed her forehead. "But why not wait until after the reading of the will?"

"Have you ever come across anything like he's talking about?"

"Never." Paige considered his question. "But if Samuel leaves Bennett his estate, he'd get the building and property, so why search now?"

"Maybe he's not so sure Samuel named him in the will."

"He is Samuel's closest relative."

"It's possible this has nothing to do with the papers."

And they were back to the beginning, without any more answers than when they started. Paige rubbed her thumb over the pillow seam as she tried to make sense of everything.

"Did any of the tenants know about Samuel's storage closet?" Jason asked.

"Not that I know of, but that doesn't mean he wouldn't tell his friends. And come to think of it, he considered most everyone in the building his friend."

"The items we packed away seemed to have more sentimental value than monetary value. Unless you were hunting for something specific and knew Samuel had it, why bother?" He raised his eyebrows. "Charlie?"

"He never showed interest in Samuel's things, but he was clearly upset to discover the doors of the unit open. And that I'd taken the boxes upstairs." Paige gasped. "Should I move the boxes to a different location? Charlie saw them in the office. He could easily go back and search each one."

He placed his thumb and forefinger over the bridge of his nose and pressed for a long moment. "It wouldn't hurt to be on the safe side. Do you have another place to store them?"

"There's a fairly empty utility room we rarely use adjacent to the office," she answered. "I could move them there."

"Charlie doesn't use it?"

"No, I keep a broom and a few cleaning supplies in there, but Charlie stores his work equipment in the basement."

"That'll work," Jason said. "Before you do that, do you mind if I go through the contents? Maybe there's a clue we missed."

Paige suddenly realized she'd been holding her breath as she waited for his advice. "You'd do that?"

"Of course. I'd do anything to protect you and Lexi." He held up a hand. "I know we haven't known each other long. I don't usually go out on a limb—"

"I don't believe that," she interrupted.

"But this time is different." Jason paused and gazed into her eyes. "You're different."

Paige didn't know how to respond.

He reached over and took her hand, then moved a few inches closer. "In the best way possible."

Touched and relieved at the same time, Paige felt tears threatening to spill down her cheeks.

Before she could muddle through her emotions, the bedroom door opened and Lexi bounded into the room. "Hey, what's for—" The teen stopped. "Sorry. I didn't know you had company."

Paige eased her hand from Jason's. "What's up?"

Lexi gaped at her mother, then ran back into her room and slammed the door.

Paige sighed and stood. "I'm sorry. This is—"

"Uncomfortable?"

She nodded. "I haven't been friends with a man since the divorce. Lexi hopes her dad and I will reconcile."

Jason's face went blank. "I should probably leave."

Paige wasn't sure if she should reassure Jason or go after her daughter. Deciding it might be best to let Lexi cool down, Paige walked with him to the door.

"The boxes," he reminded her.

She glanced at Lexi's closed door.

"If you give me the keys to the office, I'll go through the boxes and move everything to the storage room," Jason offered.

"You really don't mind?"

He held out his hand. "Trust me."

Paige hesitated. Should she? Could she?

On the other hand, did she have a choice?

Once the boxes containing Samuel's belongings were in his apartment, Jason considered his conversation with Paige. He still hadn't figured out why strange things were happening at Poinciana Arms. Right now, there were a few avenues to follow, but what was at the crux of it all? He wanted to make sure Paige and Lexi were safe. Paige might be confused about events, but she hadn't resorted to sticking her head in the sand. He admired that about her. One of many attributes he found extremely attractive.

Jason shook his head. He was getting way ahead of himself. Paige had too much on her plate to worry about his expectations. And to be honest, the idea of starting a relationship under the circumstances probably wasn't a good one. Yes, he'd dated over the years, and he'd been in a serious relationship. But he'd been single for a long time. Could Paige change that status? Did he even want her to? Or was he confusing real feelings with the intense desire to protect a single mother in a dangerous situation?

And what about Lexi? When she'd first come out of her room, he'd read her panic when she saw him. Was she worried he would tell Paige about the items she'd slipped into her backpack? Suddenly, he wondered why he hadn't said anything to Paige. Perhaps it had to do with his memories of Alyssa. He was hoping for the best in Lexi.

Then Lexi had realized that Jason and her mother were sitting close together on the couch. He'd seen the hurt and anger in the teenager's features. He knew from personal experience that it was difficult having divorced parents, but to all appearances, Paige was a great mom.

Jason thought back to those first years after his parents' divorce. He'd been furious with his dad and disappointed in his mom, but mostly worried about his sister. So he could have cut Lexi plenty of slack—if she hadn't stolen some of Samuel's belongings.

He pushed away his thoughts as his stomach started to growl. After throwing together a quick dinner, he turned on the television and ate at the small table, scanning his surroundings. His belongings were sparse, unlike Paige's colorfully decorated apartment. The lone personal touch was his lacrosse stick propped in one corner of the living room, reminding him that it had been a long time since he'd played. Paige had made her apartment a home. He'd made a place to rest his head, nothing more. He'd never considered it before, but suddenly it felt deeply unfulfilling.

Jason cleaned up, then went into the living room to examine the four boxes he'd brought into the apartment. He opened the box of books and flipped through the pages. He even checked the pasted endpapers, running his fingers over the material to see if there were any discernible lumps. He went through the rest of the boxes with the same care, but he found nothing of note.

After closing the boxes, Jason carried them to the utility room and returned Paige's keys, letting her know that everything was okay.

She nodded, then closed the door, clearly distracted. If he had to guess, she was most likely worried about Lexi.

When Jason went home, he tried to catch up on some reading, but he was unable to sit still. Instead, he called Tad Russell, the friend who had hired him when he'd retired.

Tad answered on the second ring. "What's up?"

"Sorry to bother you," Jason said. "I wanted to ask if it would be against company policy for me to do a little personal research at the office."

"It depends on what you're researching."

"You know the new apartment building I moved into?"

"Of course," Tad replied. "I'm jealous you found a vacancy before I did."

"There's sort of a situation here."

"Care to fill me in?"

Jason didn't feel right about going into specifics, so he remained vague. "I will once I get a better handle on what I'm searching for, but it's still early days."

"That doesn't sound very promising," Tad remarked. "Does this have anything to do with a gut instinct?"

"I'm afraid so."

"Then go for it," Tad said. "Make sure you keep me informed. And please, nothing out of legal bounds."

"Like I said, it's only research," Jason told him. He wanted to do basic background checks on Bennett Calhoun and Charlie Pollard.

They talked for a few more minutes, and Jason ended the call. As he set his cell phone on the desk in the living room, he noticed the drawer open a crack. It was probably nothing, but in light of his conversation with Paige, he crouched down to study the drawer more closely, inside and out. Pens, pencils, and papers were lined up exactly as he'd left them. What were the odds that he'd simply grown paranoid? Slim to none. But he'd never expected to see so many strange occurrences right after he moved in. In fact, he hadn't expected any at all.

To ease his mind, Jason scoured his apartment, but nothing was out of place. Could his usually reliable gut instinct be wrong?

He wondered what he'd gotten himself into, not sure if he should proceed into the Poinciana Arms drama. Then he pictured Paige's pale face and the pleading in her eyes. She probably didn't realize she telegraphed her fear. He shook his head, knowing he couldn't stay safely on the sidelines.

Jason moved back to the desk to close the drawer when he heard a sound that didn't quite belong. He went still, listening intently. It sounded like a scraping at the door. He scanned the room for a weapon and grabbed the lacrosse stick in the corner, then ran to the door and yanked it open.

No one stood outside his door.

He stepped into the breezeway.

Empty.

Taking a chance, Jason ran to the center of the courtyard, searching first in the direction of the street. A single car passed by. He pivoted the other way, but nothing stirred in the back area of the building.

Lowering the stick, he stood still and listened, but he didn't hear or see anything out of the ordinary. As he turned, a rustling came from the foliage a few feet away. Jason went alert, his heart racing, until Gus strolled into the halo of the overhead light.

Relief swept over Jason. "It's only you," he murmured, scratching the cat behind his ears. "I don't suppose you saw anyone out here, did you?"

Gus bumped his head against Jason's ankle.

"Yeah, that's what I thought."

The cat strolled away with his tail high in the air.

After another scan of his surroundings, Jason retreated to his apartment, checking the lock. Normal wear and tear, nothing to cause alarm.

Could Paige's fears be rubbing off on him? Or was there something more sinister happening?

Jason was determined to find out.

10

After another restless night, Paige got Lexi off to school Tuesday morning, then went to the office and booted up her computer.

A hard rap sounded on the door.

Paige jumped, and her breath stopped.

The door swung open, and a young man strolled inside. He held up a large envelope. "I need you to sign for this delivery."

It took a moment for his words to sink in. She put one hand over her rapidly beating heart and rounded the desk. She really needed to get a handle on her nerves.

The man held out the tablet, and Paige scribbled her signature on the screen with her finger. He handed her the envelope and left.

She read the return address on the envelope. It was from the office of Randall Stein, Samuel's attorney. After sliding her finger under the flap, she opened the envelope to find a letter requesting her presence at the reading of Samuel's last will and testament the following week.

Paige dropped into her chair, stunned. Samuel had included her in his last wishes? Had the dear man left her something of sentimental value? Honestly, there could be no other reason. She wasn't a relative or an investment associate. She'd merely been his employee and a friend.

Did she have the emotional strength to show up? On the other hand, going to the appointment meant she'd find out the future of the building. Bennett could say all he wanted about his ownership of the property. The attorney would have answers for everyone.

She stared at her cell phone, wanting more than anything to call Jason, except she didn't have his number. Sure, she could find his cell phone information in the papers he'd provided before signing the lease, but Paige wanted him to willingly give her the number.

After thinking long and hard, she set down the phone. No, she wouldn't become dependent on him. Yes, she liked talking to him, but she had to deal with these things herself.

She jumped at the sound of a loud bump outside.

Charlie entered the office, balancing his toolbox and a can of paint. "Sorry. Didn't mean to make so much racket."

"It's all right," Paige said as she dropped the letter on the desk.

He set the toolbox and paint on the floor, then walked over to her. "Are you okay?"

"I didn't get much sleep last night."

"Still missing Samuel?"

"I think I always will."

Charlie nodded. "You got one too?" he asked, motioning to the letter.

"Pardon?"

"A letter from the lawyer about Samuel's will."

Paige was surprised that Charlie had been invited too, but she realized it made sense. Samuel and Charlie had been friends. She was glad Charlie was going because it would be nice to have an ally on the day of the reading.

"I have no idea why he'd want me there," he remarked, pain lacing his tone.

His solemn sentence squeezed her heart. Of course Charlie missed Samuel as much as she did. Paige picked up the letter. "I've tried to come up with a reason why he'd want me there too."

"You were special to him. He always said so."

"Thanks," she whispered.

"Granted, I didn't have a close relationship with him like you did, but Samuel was a stand-up guy," Charlie said. "He gave me this job. I can't thank him enough."

Her throat grew tight.

"I want to keep my job here, so I'm not making any waves."

Did that mean he was hoping to hedge his bets with Bennett? The idea made her stomach churn.

"Any work orders besides the paint touch-ups?" he asked.

Paige shook off her suspicions and handed him the three calls that had come in that day. "Nothing major. When you finish, could you please check the parking lot gate? It's stuck again."

"We may have to call in a repairman from the manufacturer," Charlie said. "I can't get it to work properly."

"That's fine. I just want it fixed."

He scanned the work requests, then said, "I'll get started on these."

When he retrieved his toolbox, she realized it was new. The old one had been yellow, but this one gleamed silver in the fluorescent light. "Where's your toolbox?"

Charlie shrugged. "I splurged and got a new one."

"I'll miss the yellow."

"Sometimes you have to go for a change."

Paige reasoned there was nothing wrong with getting new work equipment, but since Charlie hadn't told her that Bennett had been on the property, she read all kinds of meaning into his statement—none of it encouraging.

When Charlie left, Paige focused on the letter. She tried to read between the lines of the request, but she came up blank. The thought of sitting in a room with Bennett made her cringe. The man had it out for her. Squaring her shoulders, she vowed that she wouldn't cower before him for any reason.

Not now. Not ever.

The surprising letter and the resulting mental spiral had thrown off her rhythm. Paige walked to the local coffee shop. Work could wait a few minutes while she had a cup of much-needed coffee.

The crowded shop, filled with locals who waved and called out a hearty good morning, went a long way toward calming her mind. Between worrying over the strange goings-on around the complex and her daughter's anger after Jason left last night, she'd tumbled into overload.

Settling in at a sidewalk table, Paige inhaled the bracing aroma of coffee, allowing the peace of the moment to wash over her. The sun warmed her shoulders, and a mild breeze lifted strands of hair from her forehead. The air held a hint of humidity and the subtle scents of salt water and damp sand—yet another reason she loved living here.

Once centered, Paige took a notepad from her purse and studied the new list of pros and cons she'd started last night when she couldn't sleep. The two columns should have been filled with words to either soothe or put her on guard. Unfortunately, her old trick of trying to control her surroundings by making lists had stopped working.

A sharp bark at her feet pulled her from her thoughts. Muffin, a polka-dot bow perched on her head, demanded her attention.

"So sorry," Mrs. Nelson said, hurrying over to Paige as the dog pulled at the end of the leash. "We were out for our morning stroll when Muffin saw you."

Paige leaned down to rub the dog's fur, smiling when Muffin wagged her tail enthusiastically.

Mrs. Nelson pointed to the empty chair. "Do you mind?"

"Please have a seat."

"Thank you," Mrs. Nelson said as she sat down. "We walked longer than usual this morning, and I need a little rest."

Paige glanced over at the marina. The boats bobbed in the waves. The sky, so blue and clear, made her squint against the brightness. "I imagine you couldn't resist being out on this beautiful day." She reached for her cup, then stopped. "Can I get you a coffee?"

"You're sweet to offer, but I already indulged." Mrs. Nelson grinned. "I rise much too early these days as it is. I really should give up caffeine."

Paige took a sip. "It's hard to give up something we like, isn't it?"

Mrs. Nelson watched her with a knowing smile. "You mean as you seem to like that handsome young man who moved in next door to you?"

Paige felt her cheeks heat and blamed it on the hot beverage. "Jason's a nice guy."

"I'd bet Muffin's favorite treats that he's caught your fancy. In the years I've known you, you've never gone out on a single date."

Paige cringed. One of the problems of living in a close community was that everyone knew her business. "I've been busy." She paused. "Lexi's not exactly ready for me to date."

To say Lexi had been upset to see her and Jason so close together on the couch was an understatement. Paige didn't blame her. She'd never shown an interest in anyone since the divorce. Paige had tried to explain to Lexi that she'd merely confided in Jason about some troubling things around the complex, and Jason had offered comfort. Lexi had been too angry to ask what troubling things Paige meant, so at least she'd dodged sharing her fears with her daughter for the time being. Knowing Lexi, that luck wouldn't hold for long.

"I understand." Sympathy flickered in Mrs. Nelson's gaze. "Divorce is never easy."

"It's a tricky road to navigate," Paige agreed. "Lexi misses her dad, and she wants us to get back together. That isn't going to happen, but I worry that Kevin might challenge the custody agreement."

Mrs. Nelson frowned. "I didn't realize custody was an issue."

"I make sure Lexi has her dedicated weeks to stay with her father during the summer, but we still revisit the issue at times. Much more than I'd like." Paige still worried what Kevin would say if he found out that someone might be prowling around the complex. One more thing keeping her awake at night.

"Lexi told me she might get a job," Mrs. Nelson said, adjusting Muffin's leash.

"She desperately wants one," Paige said. "I've offered her odd jobs around the building, but I can't compete with something of her own."

A picture of Lexi's new shoes flashed in Paige's mind. Perhaps Lexi's push for regular hours came from a desire to buy more designer clothes?

"I suppose that means she'll have less time to watch Muffin." Mrs. Nelson leaned down and scooped up the dog. "We'll miss her, won't we?"

Paige grinned. She loved that the older woman spoiled her canine companion.

After drowning the dog in compliments, Mrs. Nelson sent Paige a sheepish grin. "I know I go overboard, but Muffin is all I have."

A shot of sadness filled Paige. "No, you have all of us at Poinciana Arms."

She noticed the sheen in the older woman's eyes, and she was grateful that Mrs. Nelson had a home and neighbors who cared for her.

"I owe you an apology," Mrs. Nelson said.

Paige tipped her head to the side. "For what?"

"Blaming you for letting someone into my apartment. Charlie assured me that he and Muffin must have been the culprits who moved my belongings around."

Paige should have been relieved, but on the heels of other problems around the property, she didn't know how to respond. "It's okay. Please promise to keep your door locked. You can never be too careful."

"Around here?" Mrs. Nelson made a tsking sound. "I've never been safer."

Paige had shared that sentiment until a few days ago. "Humor me."

Mrs. Nelson laughed. "I promise." She stood, settling Muffin in her arms. "We should get home. Thank you for indulging me for a few minutes."

"Anytime." Paige watched as Muffin jumped down and led Mrs. Nelson down the sidewalk.

The older woman waved, Muffin barked, and everything was as it should be.

Except it wasn't, and Paige couldn't forget that.

With a sigh, she closed the notebook and drained her coffee. She had work to do. Tossing the cup in a nearby trash can, she made her way back to the complex. The streets were bustling. The spring tourists were always a boost for this beach town. The local merchants and restaurateurs stayed busy, and it was beneficial for everyone.

Paige didn't want to leave Peters Cove. So what would she do if the new owners of Poinciana Arms let her go after the reading of Samuel's will? The thought tore at her heart. She waved to store owners along her walk, realizing that this town had truly become home. She wanted a permanent life here with Lexi.

Paige decided she'd cross that bridge when she got to it. Thanks to Samuel, she now had three years of management experience. Surely she could find another position if necessary.

She reached the gimmicky gift store Lexi loved. Suddenly she was struck by a strong sense of being followed. As she passed the store, she caught sight of the reflection in the display window and spotted a figure closing in behind her. Panic made her increase her step. Was she imagining things? Again? There were still plenty of people around her as she walked to the residential area, so why was she so afraid?

That prickly sensation at the back of her neck intensified.

Clutching her purse, Paige hurried down the sidewalk and around the corner at the end of the block. She glanced over her shoulder, but no one seemed out of place. Still, the intensity wouldn't subside. Almost jogging now, she moved as fast as she dared without looking ridiculous and made it to the apartment building in no time. As she rushed to the office, she peeked over her shoulder again and glimpsed the empty sidewalk. Had she been wrong?

Berating herself for worrying over nothing and ruining her pleasant morning, Paige unlocked the office. She tossed her purse in the bottom desk drawer, then pulled up a program on her computer with shaking fingers.

"Stop," she muttered to herself.

But her mind kept spinning. What were the odds of thinking she was being followed on the same day she received a letter about Samuel's last testament? About as great as someone snooping around the basement and making threatening phone calls. None of this made sense. Paige was merely the apartment manager. She wasn't in line to inherit Samuel's assets. Everyone knew the two of them had been friends.

So who had it out for her? And why?

By late afternoon, Paige went to the apartment, ready to kick off her shoes and put her feet up. She considered ordering takeout tonight so she wouldn't have to cook. It sounded heavenly.

"What do you want for dinner?" she called out to Lexi.

Silence filtered through the apartment.

Paige went to her daughter's room and knocked. When she didn't get a response, she opened the door. The room was empty.

She checked her watch. It was 5:15. Lexi was always home from school by now.

Don't panic, Paige thought as she returned to the living room.

Suddenly, the door opened, and Lexi strode inside, sparkly backpack over her shoulder. There were fuchsia streaks in her pretty blonde hair.

Speechless, she stared at her daughter.

"What?" Lexi demanded.

"Your hair."

"I wanted something different," Lexi said.

"Well, you certainly succeeded," Paige responded.

Lexi glared at her. "You don't like it?"

"It's a surprise," Paige said. "You didn't talk to me about a change."

"It's my hair."

Paige refused to get into an argument over color that would grow out. No, her daughter's sullen attitude worried her more. "Where did you get it done?"

"A friend's mom works in a salon. She did it for us."

"Okay," Paige said, making a mental note to ask Lexi more about her friend later. "But how did you pay for it?"

"I don't always have to ask you for money," Lexi replied. "I have my own."

"From watching Muffin?"

"And other stuff."

"What other stuff?" Paige persisted.

"None of your business, okay?" Lexi stormed off to her bedroom. The key dangling from her backpack hit the doorjamb, and then she slammed the door.

What was going on with her daughter? Paige wanted to teach Lexi independence, and she encouraged her to spread her wings. But this felt more like anger rather than trying new things. Could the hair color have anything to do with Paige spending time with Jason? Was Lexi acting out?

Paige thought back to Lexi telling her about hanging out with friends Paige didn't know. Were they bad influences? And once again Paige wondered where Lexi had gotten the money.

A horrifying thought occurred to her. Could Lexi be the one breaking into tenants' apartments? But how? Was she stealing things to get extra money for expensive shoes and salon-quality color? What other surprises did Lexi have locked up in her bedroom that Paige didn't know about?

And how awful of Paige to assume the worst of her child.

Was it time to bring Kevin into the situation? As much as Paige didn't want to tell him, he was Lexi's father, and he had the right to know. He might have insight that Paige didn't.

Mind whirling, Paige moved to the counter where she'd left her phone, then paused. Lexi couldn't get into the apartments unaided because each apartment key fob could only be activated by the app on Paige's phone. Plus, the password protection ensured its safety.

Could Lexi have taken her phone without Paige's knowledge? Maybe late at night while Paige slept? If Lexi cracked the pass code, once she walked to a door, the app would open it. But Lexi had to know her password. Paige had never mentioned it. Nor had Lexi ever expressed any interest in how the locks at each apartment door worked. No, there had to be something else going on.

Paige felt pain radiating up her jaw and realized she'd been clenching her teeth. She grabbed her phone and moved out of earshot of her daughter as she made the dreaded phone call to her ex-husband.

Jason arrived at Poinciana Arms, glad to be home. A new project had come in, and Tad made him the lead. Jason always enjoyed diving into something new, but it left him little time to do background checks on Bennett and Charlie.

The gate to the parking lot was stuck open. Jason was surprised the problem hadn't been fixed, so he parked and headed to the pole to check it out. He followed the end of the bar to where it attached to the pole mechanism and noticed wires hanging out. He lifted them and discovered they'd been severed. The cuts were too neat to have been an accident.

As Jason walked through the courtyard, he saw Paige leaving her apartment. His mood instantly improved at the sight of his lovely neighbor, despite the news he was about to deliver.

"I'm glad I caught you," he called out. "Did you know the parking lot gate wires were cut?"

Paige glanced up from her phone. "The what?"

"The gate," Jason said, then explained what he'd found.

"I asked Charlie to check it out," she said, "but he never got back to me."

"Maybe he's in the process of fixing it."

"He did mention that we might have to call the manufacturer." Paige bit her lip. "Or someone tampered with it to remind me of what's going on around here."

"I hope that's not the case," he said.

She ran a hand over her brow. "I'll have to deal with it later, but right now I have more pressing matters to take care of."

"What's wrong?" Jason asked, concerned.

"Oh, nothing. I was trying to make a phone call. I need to touch base with my ex-husband, Kevin, about Lexi."

"I'm sorry," he said. "I didn't mean to pry."

"It's okay," Paige said. "I'm just stressed out about everything—the weird stuff going on around here, possibly getting fired when the new owner takes over this place, my daughter—all of it."

"Let's sit down and talk for a minute." Jason led her to the bench in the courtyard located near the fountain, and they sat down. "First of all, no one is going to fire you."

She snorted.

"But with that attitude, I might be wrong," he teased.

Paige gave him a weak smile, then said, "I've been asked to attend the reading of Samuel's will."

Jason wasn't surprised. Paige had spoken so highly of Samuel and their friendship. "And?"

"I guess I'll find out my future for sure."

"Then you'll know where you stand, and you can make a plan," he told her. "I've seen you handle quite a bit since we've met. No matter what's thrown at you, I know you'll come out stronger."

"It seems appropriate that I receive a pep talk from the man who ran into the basement with me when the alarm went off *and* chased an intruder out the door."

"Okay, so that was unusual," Jason admitted. "And the other events may not be related."

"You don't believe that."

"No, I don't." He was pretty sure he'd heard someone other than the cat at his door last night. Bennett was the first suspect on his list. "What's really going on?"

She pressed her lips together and remained silent.

Jason decided to try another tactic. "Don't forget that I moved into this complex even with all kinds of weird things going on. I think I'm up to hearing what's bothering you."

"And make me sound even more pathetic?" Paige crossed her arms over her chest. "No thank you."

"You had a shock when Samuel died," he reminded her. "I'd be surprised if you weren't affected more than you realize."

She wiped tears from her eyes. "Do you think so?"

"I know so." Jason stretched his arm out on the bench behind Paige, tempted to place his hand on her shoulder to comfort her, but he held back. "My sister, Alyssa, was in and out of trouble all the time when we were kids. My parents didn't make the situation any better. They judged her without providing any real help. So that left me to keep Alyssa safe. When I went away to college, I thought I'd finally be able to live for myself. But Alyssa became involved with a rough crowd and got arrested. By then, my parents had washed their hands of her."

"But you couldn't."

"No." He thought back to those days when he'd tried so hard to make a difference in Alyssa's life. How he'd encouraged her to turn her life around. How he'd lived with the heartache of trying to protect a person who didn't want to be protected.

"What happened after that?" Paige asked, compassion in her tone.

"She took off. I searched everywhere for her, but I didn't have any resources back then. I mean, I was a kid in college. What did I know about investigating a disappearance?"

"Did you find her?"

"No, the police did." Jason paused. "She died from a drug overdose."

Paige gasped. "Oh no. I'm so sorry."

He moved his arm from behind Paige, then rested his elbows on his knees and hung his head. Even after all these years, it still hurt to talk about his lost sister. "I blamed myself for a long time, and I did my own share of grieving."

Sorrow etched her face. "Was that why you encouraged me to remember the special times after I'd told you about Samuel's funeral?"

Jason nodded. "Sometimes I feel like it's the best way I can make sense of what happened to Alyssa."

"It's good advice, but I'm sorry you had to go through such a tragedy to learn it," Paige said. "Was that the reason why you joined the military?"

"Partly. I needed a change, and that's as big as it comes. Once I got into intelligence, I realized it had a lot to do with Alyssa."

"It also explains why you offered to watch out for Lexi and me."

"All part of the neighborly service."

"You must think I'm clueless," she muttered, tucking a strand of hair behind her ear.

He studied her. "What I see is a great mom and an attractive woman, working hard to make a decent life for her family."

"The mom thing, not so much."

"Why would you say that?" Jason asked, surprised.

"My daughter came home today with fuchsia streaks in her hair," Paige announced with a grimace.

He blinked. "No wonder you're stressed out."

"Yes, and I'm wishing my sweet baby girl wouldn't grow up so fast."

Jason shook his head. "I have to admit, understanding kids is not in my realm of expertise."

Paige leaned close, her shoulder brushing his. "Trust me, raising a child is on-the-job training every single day."

He savored her closeness, honored that she took comfort from leaning against him. Perhaps even trusted him.

Jason pushed away those thoughts and said, "Sometimes what you need is a big scoop of ice cream to make everything okay. That's what Alyssa and I would do when things were out of control."

Paige grinned. "Sounds delicious." Her smile quickly faded. "But I'd rather have answers. Excuse me for a minute." She rose and walked a few steps away to place a call.

He heard her leave a message for Kevin. Again, Jason admired that Paige put Lexi first. Talking to her ex-husband might not be comfortable, but Paige didn't shy away from the heavy lifting. It made him like her even more.

Paige returned to the bench, and they sat in silence for a while, the gurgling fountain their sole companion.

Jason relished her nearness. He liked that they were in this situation together, even if they had no clue what was going on or why. If Paige wanted answers, he'd help her get them. "I have an idea. Why not do some research?"

She straightened. "What do you have in mind?"

"You're concerned about the possible sale of the property," he reminded her. "Samuel's nephew hinted that he would soon be the owner. See a theme?"

Her eyes lit up. "When you put it that way, I do."

"So we follow that lead."

"I've never dug too much into the history of the property," Paige admitted. "I never needed to. I only did some basic research when I first started working here because I was curious, and I wanted a little historical background about my new home."

"But now there's more motivation," he said.

She gazed across the courtyard, obviously lost in thought. Finally, she turned to him. "My mother once said that if you go snooping into other people's secrets, you're likely to find things you wish you hadn't."

"Or you learn facts that play to your advantage," Jason countered.

Paige took a deep breath. "Okay, I'm in."

"How about tomorrow?" he suggested. "We can do an online search to start. Maybe that'll give us what we need."

"Samuel's will won't be read until next week," she said.

"You'd probably feel better if you had an idea of what's at stake," Jason said. "How about we meet at your office after lunch? I can go into work for half a day."

"Are you sure? I don't want this to affect your job. This is my problem, not yours."

"I'd like to make it our problem." He took her hand and squeezed it.

"Thank you." Paige smiled at him.

Her radiant expression made his chest grow tight.

All of a sudden, she cleared her throat, removed her hand from his, and stood. "I need to get back to Lexi. Hopefully, there won't be any change in tomorrow's plan."

"Just in case, let me give you my number," Jason said.

After they'd exchanged numbers, she said, "Looks like we're covered now." With a wave, she headed to her apartment.

As he watched her go, he realized Paige hadn't told him why she needed to call her ex-husband. Surely she could handle her daughter's fuchsia hair, right? Or was there something more serious going on that she hadn't mentioned?

Guilt swept over Jason. He hadn't been completely straightforward with her either. He neglected to mention that he'd seen Lexi swiping a few of Samuel's things. He reasoned that he needed more time to figure out Lexi's motivation.

Now he hoped his silence wouldn't backfire on him.

After lunch the next day, Paige sat beside Jason at her desk and pulled up the website for the county property appraiser on her computer.

He handed her a stack of papers. "I went to the site last night and downloaded and printed information we might be able to use."

"Nothing like thinking ahead." She tapped her pen against a notepad. "I made a list of topics we should research. I'll compare them to what you found."

They divided the papers and got to work.

When Paige read the value of the land and apartment building, her jaw dropped. "There are a lot of zeros in that number."

"I'm not surprised," Jason said. "Property values are increasing as more people move here."

"That explains why Bennett so desperately wants ownership. It also explains why Mason has a buyer lined up."

"Have you heard back from him?"

She shook her head. "Not since he informed me about the appraisal. I'm wondering if he's waiting to see what happens with Samuel's will."

"He can't do much until then," he pointed out.

"Still, he's not a man who takes no for an answer," Paige said. "He'll find a way to expedite the sale."

They spent the next thirty minutes scouring the parcel numbers, property records, and tax assessments.

She rubbed her blurry eyes, then peered at Jason as he compared two pieces of paper. He appeared so serious and in control. She found his calmness appealing. It was the opposite of what she was feeling. "Did you find something?"

"Maybe. When did you say the property was originally purchased?"

Paige sifted through the stack of papers to find the answer. "It was 1935." She dropped the paper. "Purchased by Richard Bishop and Colin Masters."

He checked his paper. "Bishop is listed but not Masters."

"That can't be right. It has to be both men, because Samuel later bought the property from Colin Masters."

"The records aren't very detailed."

She frowned. "Really? That's surprising."

"It's definitely strange."

Paige set her elbow on the desk and rested her chin in her palm. "If the records list Bishop's name alone, there might be credence to Bennett's claim." The idea chilled her. "So what are we missing?"

"It all comes back to Samuel and his wishes for the property." Jason went through the papers again. "Since you mentioned that Samuel's accountant wanted an appraisal, I checked for recent requests. I found one from six months ago."

"Who made the request?"

"It doesn't give that info."

"Samuel?"

"Most likely," he answered. "Did he have some kind of plans for the building?"

"Not that I'm aware of." She thought back to their conversations. "Wait a minute. I remember Samuel mentioning the National Register."

"Did he want to make Poinciana Arms a historical landmark?"

"I don't know. He said it in passing."

Jason tapped on the keyboard. "There's a state preservation office in the county building. Let's go see what we can find."

"Sounds good."

"I'll meet you at my car." He grabbed his keys and left.

Paige collected all the data and stowed it in her desk drawer. Her phone rang, startling her, and she checked the caller ID. It was Samuel's accountant.

"I wanted you to know that Samuel's will is going to be read on Monday," Mason said.

"I'm aware," she responded. "I've been requested to attend the reading."

There was a moment of silence before he spoke. "I didn't realize."

"It came as a shock to me as well," Paige admitted. "I can't imagine why he'd want me there."

"We all recognized your friendship with Samuel," Mason said. "But don't worry. You won't be alone. I'll be there as well. It'll be nice to see a familiar face."

"Thank you," she said.

"If you need anything, please let me know," he said, compassion in his voice. "I know this is very difficult for you."

"I appreciate it," Paige said.

After disconnecting the call, she locked the office and dropped her keys and phone into her purse, then met Jason in the parking lot.

As he drove to their destination, Paige told him about Mason's call.

Jason glanced at her. "Hopefully, once the question of ownership is settled, you'll only have apartment management to keep you busy."

She hoped he was right.

When they arrived at the preservation office, the woman behind the counter smiled at them. She had stylish gray hair, and a pair of bifocals hung from a gold chain around her neck. "Good afternoon. I'm Bea. How can I assist you?"

"I'm hoping you can help us with some information about Poinciana Arms," Paige replied, then gave the woman the address.

Bea set her glasses on her nose. "Are you searching as an agent of the estate?"

Unsure how to respond, Paige glanced at Jason.

He nodded.

Paige said to Bea, "I work there for Samuel Bishop."

Bea's smile brightened. "I haven't seen Samuel in some time. How is he doing?"

"Then you haven't heard," Paige said.

The woman peered over her bifocals. "Heard?"

"I'm sorry to tell you that Samuel passed away," Paige said softly. She hated to be the bearer of bad news. "It was a car accident."

"Oh my goodness," Bea said, placing a hand over her heart. "I don't know what to say."

"It was a shock to everyone," Paige said.

"I haven't seen Samuel since he started the arrangements to have Poinciana Arms made into a historical landmark," Bea commented. "Once the process got underway, he couldn't hide his excitement. He said he wanted to make sure the property remained the way he'd intended."

But he kept it from me, Paige thought, hurt. She wondered why he didn't tell her if he was so excited about it.

"If you don't mind my asking," Jason said to Bea, "how far did Samuel get in the process?"

"Samuel had already established the age, significance, and integrity of the building for the criteria for evaluation," Bea replied. "The next step to move forward involved listing the property in the register."

"But he never got any further," Paige whispered, a wave of grief crashing over her. Would it ever go away?

Bea shook her head. "I'm afraid not."

Jason rested his hand on Paige's shoulder.

Paige took strength from his comforting presence.

"He ran into a problem," Bea told them. "Apparently there were ownership discrepancies. The property is listed under one owner, but Samuel insisted it was a joint purchase."

"Is that unusual?" Jason asked.

"It's hard to say, but the issue needed to be cleared up before Samuel could proceed," Bea answered. "He told me he'd check into what he thought might be additional ownership documents."

"Back to the old drawing board," Paige muttered under her breath.

"May I ask who will be continuing with the process?" Bea asked.

"I don't have an answer for that yet," Paige said, worried more than ever about the outcome of Samuel's will. Would the new owners honor his wishes?

"Please let me know if I can do anything to help," Bea offered.

"Thank you," Paige said, even though things were muddier than when they'd started their quest for answers.

"Do you happen to have the original blueprints?" Jason asked.

"You can get them at the property appraiser's office," Bea said. "Although you aren't the first to ask about Poinciana Arms. Besides Samuel, that is."

Paige leaned closer to the counter. "Someone else requested information?"

"Yes, he was a big man," Bea said. "Looked like he worked out a lot. Kind of straggly black hair."

"Charlie?" Paige asked, a sinking feeling in the pit of her stomach.

"I didn't get his name," Bea said. "He came in to pick up some papers for Samuel. A copy of the original building permits, if I remember correctly."

Paige glanced at Jason, the same surprise reflected in his eyes. "Recently?"

"No," Bea said. "It was around the time Samuel made the initial inquiries about the process."

"Thanks for your assistance," Jason said to Bea, then caught Paige by the elbow and ushered her outside.

"Okay, that was strange," Paige blurted as soon as they made it to the parking lot. The late afternoon sun hung high in the sky, hot enough to warm her shoulders, which she needed after the chill of learning Charlie had been here nosing around.

"You really didn't know anything about Samuel's plans?" Jason asked as they walked to his car.

"No. I mean, he always said he had special plans for the property, but he never gave me any specifics."

Her phone beeped, and Paige saw a text from Lexi. *Having dinner at Tina's tonight. Can I sleep over?*

Normally, Paige would have hesitated to grant permission for a school night sleepover. But at this point, having Lexi off the property made Paige feel like she was keeping her daughter safe. She'd finally discussed Lexi's behavior with Kevin, leaving out the unusual events around the complex for now. He knew about Lexi applying for the job and was happy to work their vacation dates around her schedule if she got the position. He'd also assured her that Lexi's moods and behavior were normal for a teenager, especially one who was taking her parents' divorce hard, which went a long way toward easing Paige's mind.

Sure, Paige texted her daughter. *Have fun.*

"Everything okay?" Jason asked.

"That was Lexi." She sighed. "I'm on my own tonight."

He moved a bit closer. She could feel his body heat and his strength, and she found herself wishing they were walking together under different circumstances. Romantic circumstances.

"I don't feel like cooking tonight," he said. "Do you want to grab some dinner so we can talk?"

Paige reined in her hopes and calmed her speeding heart. They'd go to dinner to talk, not start a relationship. Not with her current problems. "I'd like that."

Jason drove back to Poinciana Arms and parked. Then they walked a few blocks to the main thoroughfare, stopping at an Italian restaurant Paige recommended.

When they were seated on the outdoor patio, Paige watched a waiter carry plates filled with pasta to a couple at a nearby table, then inhaled the scent of zesty spices that hung in the air. She savored the salty breeze on her face, enjoying the peace after all the turmoil of late. "I feel like this is the calm before the storm."

"You were awfully quiet on the way home," Jason remarked as he shook out the napkin and placed it over his lap.

"I'm trying to put all this together."

"It is rather like a puzzle."

She wrinkled her nose. "Not a fan."

Jason chuckled. "Noted."

The waiter came by and took their drink orders.

"Something is really bothering me," she said after the young man left.

"Let me guess," Jason said. "If Samuel was in the process of making Poinciana Arms a historic landmark, then there's no way he'd consider selling."

"Exactly." She watched the bustling sidewalk with a touch of envy. People were taking advantage of the temperate weather to enjoy the evening. What she wouldn't give for this to be a normal night, a normal dinner, without all the questions flying around. "Could Samuel have forgotten to tell Mason that he'd changed his mind?"

Jason rested his elbows on the cloth-covered table. "Or could Mason be working with someone who expects to inherit the property?"

"I doubt it," Paige said. "Mason was very adamant that Samuel told him to handle prospective buyers. But now, we don't know who the owners will be."

"Regardless, it doesn't seem like Samuel intended to sell. Maybe he simply didn't get the chance to tell Mason before he died."

She let her gaze wander up and down the street, admiring the old-fashioned lampposts, the eclectic architecture of the buildings, and the businesses that had been here for generations. This town had become home. A sense of belonging washed over her, and she dared a glance at the man seated across from her. Would he feel that way someday too?

He focused on the menu, the light from the flickering candle dancing over his handsome features.

Jason was there for Paige in a way she'd never expected. But did they share the same interests and outlooks on life? So far, she'd say yes, but again, this wasn't a date, much to her disappointment. Should she keep hoping that their relationship might become more than solely searching for answers? Once the questions were answered, would Jason return to his old life as if nothing had happened?

Shaking off her secret yearning, Paige got back on track. "Samuel was disappointed that the town was becoming more industrial. He loved the old buildings and their original character, and he absolutely hated the uninspired high-rises popping up."

The waiter delivered their beverages, and they placed their orders. Paige chose bucatini with butter-roasted tomato sauce, and Jason selected chicken fettuccine Alfredo.

When they were alone again, Jason focused on her, his eyes gleaming.

Paige felt herself blush at his attention. She hoped he didn't notice.

"Okay, here's a question," he said. "What is Charlie's role in this?"

In the blink of an eye, the magic was gone, reminding her that this was not a night on the town. They had more important things to discuss.

"I've been thinking about that," Paige said. "Bea mentioned he stopped at the preservation office for Samuel a while ago. Perhaps Samuel included Charlie in his plans."

"But not you?"

She couldn't deny that it stung to know that Samuel had confided in Charlie but not her. "I can't come up with any other conclusion. Charlie always ran errands or did odd jobs for Samuel. He must have trusted Charlie."

"Do you trust Charlie?" Jason asked.

"I used to, but I'm not so sure anymore." Paige sighed. "The reading of the will can't come soon enough."

"I agree." He leaned back in his chair. "I'm planning to run background checks on Charlie and Bennett. We need to know as much as possible about them."

The waiter delivered their meals. Paige and Jason focused on their savory pasta dishes, taking a brief break from their discussion.

When Paige had eaten her fill, she pushed her plate aside. "Here's another question. Bea mentioned a problem with the original ownership papers. We'd already established that. But what if there are two copies? What if Bennett is right somehow?"

Jason set his fork down. "Are you saying that his mother should have inherited the property?"

"If there isn't a tie to Colin Masters on the original ownership papers, does that mean he didn't have legal ownership of the property along with Richard Bishop?" she asked. "And in that case, what do we do about the fact Samuel bought it from Masters if Masters never legally owned the property? Does the sale become null and void? What if Bennett can prove his mother's claim?"

He frowned. "Then we need to find those papers."

Paige tossed her napkin on the table, her stomach in knots. "Do you mind if we settle up and head home?"

"Of course not." Jason waved down the waiter and requested the check.

When it arrived, Paige fished in her purse for her wallet, but Jason pulled out his credit card. "It's my treat," he said.

"You don't have to pay for my meal," she protested.

"I want to."

Her cheeks heated. She briefly allowed herself the fantasy that this handsome man had dined with her because he found her attractive, not simply to discuss troubling events. Now they would go back to the apartment and—what? Share a good-night kiss?

Paige shook off the image, calling herself foolish, afraid Jason would read her emotions. He was much too perceptive. Most likely he felt sorry for the predicament she found herself in. She recalled their conversation and how he'd taken care of his sister. Clearly, Jason had a strong protective streak.

They were quiet during the walk back to the apartment building. Paige was lost in her own thoughts, and she assumed Jason was too.

"Thanks for dinner," she said when they stepped into the courtyard.

He smiled. "It was my pleasure."

"Are you sure you don't have second thoughts about this friendship?" Paige asked, trying for a light tone.

"Why?" Jason asked. "Do you not need a friend?"

"No, it's not that," she said. "Since you moved in, I've taken up a hefty chunk of your time."

"I wouldn't have it any other way," he said.

But did she want it this way? Would Jason stick around once they'd figured out why strange things were happening to her? She didn't want to think about it. The exhaustion of the day was catching up to her. "I'm glad. And I'm going to call it a night."

Jason nodded. "Get a good night's sleep. We'll regroup tomorrow."

She smiled, then nearly ran to her door. Once inside, she placed her purse on the counter and brushed a hand through her hair. Spending time with Jason was becoming as confusing as attempting to figure out what would become of Poinciana Arms.

With a shake of her head, which made the thoughts rattling around even worse, Paige flipped off the light in the kitchen. She dreaded being alone tonight, but she couldn't deny her relief that Lexi was safe.

As she switched off the lamp beside the couch, she noticed a motion outside the window. She crept close, thinking it might have been the wind in the trees, then gasped.

A figure crouched low, moving along the side of the building.

13

Jason was heading to his bedroom when a frantic knocking rattled his door. He rushed to the door and opened it.

Paige stood there, her face pale in the breezeway lighting. "There's someone lurking outside my window." Before he could respond, she grabbed his hand, tugging him into the courtyard.

"Wait a second," Jason protested.

"No time," Paige said. Her hand trembled in his. "Whoever it is will get away."

He matched her pace as they ran around the side of the building.

Night blanketed the sky in shades of purple and navy. Streetlights burned, the light casting shadows over the manicured lawn. Salt tinted the air, the humidity making it all the more noticeable.

Paige slid to an abrupt stop, her labored breathing echoing unusually loud in the quiet night, and released his hand.

Jason halted beside her. "What is it?" he asked, scanning the area for threats.

"I swear I saw someone outside my window." The conviction in her voice erased any doubts. "I went to turn off the lamp and noticed a figure moving along the building."

As his eyes adjusted to the dim lighting, he didn't see a figure crouching in the shadows or a shape running in the distance. Everything seemed calm. "Could it have been car lights bouncing off the shrubs?"

"No, it was a figure," Paige insisted. "I'm sure of it."

"Man? Woman?"

"I couldn't tell," she said. "The person moved too fast."

"Hold on." With measured steps, Jason walked the property along the building. While he didn't doubt Paige, she'd encountered more than her share of suspicious events lately, and she was one step away from exhaustion. Maybe her mind was playing tricks on her.

When he returned to Paige, he said, "I didn't see anyone."

Her shoulders slumped. "Just my luck."

His heart ached at her dejected expression. "Let's walk around the perimeter."

"Why? The person is probably long gone."

"It'll make me feel better," Jason said evenly, hoping it would calm her nerves if she started moving again.

Paige fell into step beside him. They walked along the rear of the property. No one jumped out to startle them. Not even Gus made an appearance. They rounded the far side by the parking lot. No shadowy figures were hiding behind the cars.

When they arrived at the front of the building, they paused on the sidewalk.

Paige scrutinized the three-story structure before them. "When I took this job, I felt like Lexi and I had finally found a home. This place and Samuel's trust in me meant so much."

"It's not over," he reminded her.

"That's not my point," she said. "These last few days have given me an insight into why men and women join the military. Why my parents and ex-husband found their jobs so important." She gestured to the building. "Poinciana Arms is worth protecting."

"I couldn't have said it better myself."

Paige gazed at him, the streetlight reflected in her eyes. "I have no idea what the future will bring, but as long as I'm here, I have to protect my home. The place where Lexi can grow up safely." Her voice softened. "The place where I met you."

Jason's breath lodged in his chest. He longed to pull her in for a kiss, but did he dare?

A car zoomed by, interrupting the intimate moment.

Paige jumped and looked away. "Once again I've led you on a chase that came up empty."

"I'm glad you feel you can come to me," Jason said. "No matter the circumstances."

"I know I saw someone outside my window," she insisted.

"Let's check one more time."

They reexamined the area near her window, investigating the best they could in the dim lighting.

"We'd probably be better off searching in the daylight tomorrow," he said.

"You're right. This is—ouch!"

"Are you okay?"

"I hit my foot on something." Paige knelt down, feeling around in the grass.

Jason joined her, his fingers closing over cool steel. He lifted it and held it in the light so he could see it better.

"What is it?"

He pointed to the hook at the end. "A pry bar."

"That's strange. We haven't had any construction going on around here," she said. "Well, except for Charlie replacing Mrs. Nelson's flooring."

"He would need a tool like this."

They stood.

"I don't think the person outside my window was Charlie," Paige remarked.

Jason glanced around the neighborhood, pry bar in hand.

"What are you thinking?" she asked, her voice shaky.

"That I need to run those background checks on Charlie and Bennett as soon as possible."

Paige motioned to the tool. "What about that?"

"I'll hold on to it for now." Jason noticed that she was shivering. "Let's get back inside."

In silence, they returned to the courtyard.

"I'm so thankful Lexi is sleeping over at Tina's." Paige ran her hands up and down her arms. "I'm not going to mention it to her. There's no need to worry her until we know what's going on."

"But—"

She held up her hand. "I know. I need to keep better tabs on her."

"Yes, but that's not what I was going to say," he responded.

She bit her lip, then said, "I realize things may seem out of control with her, but she's a good kid. What she's going through is normal teenage stuff."

Jason certainly didn't have the expertise of raising a child, and voicing his concerns might be interpreted as stepping over the line. "Are you sure?"

Paige nodded. "Kevin and I discussed it, and we're on the same page."

He knew it was the end of the discussion. He wasn't the dad here. His opinion didn't matter to Paige, even though he wished otherwise. "I'll leave it in your capable hands."

She laughed. "Thanks for the vote of confidence."

They made it to her door. Jason wanted to say more and figure out a better way to protect her, but she'd grown calmer now, and he didn't want to upset her again by mentioning security measures. She probably didn't need him after all.

"Hopefully, this ends the excitement for tonight," Paige said.

"I'm right—"

"Next door." She grinned. "I know."

He gripped the pry bar in his hand. "Try to get some sleep."

Paige sent him a wobbly smile. "You too." Then she went inside and closed the door quietly.

Jason stood there, listening for anything out of the ordinary. The gurgle of the fountain was all that broke the silence. It appeared to be a normal night at Poinciana Arms.

But whatever was going on here was far from normal.

The next few days were surprisingly uneventful. Paige managed to get through the hours without any bizarre events intruding on her life. Lexi acted a little more like her old self, which gave Paige hope. Jason spent long hours at work, so she hadn't seen him much. She told herself she didn't miss him, but it was a lie.

On Monday morning, Paige tumbled out of bed, her stomach in knots. Today was the reading of Samuel's will. She was anxious to hear what it said, but she was also a nervous wreck.

After Lexi left for school, Paige dressed in a navy suit with a yellow silk top. She arranged her hair in a tight chignon for a more professional look.

She arrived at the attorney's office, prepared for the worst. Her stomach continued to churn. The cool and quiet interior—a direct contrast to the blazing sunshine and traffic outside—did wonders for her nerves. Paige regarded the lobby, impressed by the elegant decor. Of course Samuel had chosen not only an efficient lawyer but one with outstanding taste as well.

Paige approached the receptionist at the front desk. "I'm here about the reading of Samuel Bishop's will."

"The gathering is in the conference room on the right," the receptionist said, motioning toward a hallway.

Paige thanked her, then headed in that direction. Her footsteps were muffled by the thick carpet, but she heard voices the closer she drew near. She stopped in the doorway. The large room held a long conference table. The floor-to-ceiling windows overlooked a serene garden, probably planted for that exact ambience.

Mason Trembly and Bennett Calhoun stood on opposite ends of the room. Other family members she recalled seeing at Samuel's funeral milled about.

Mason approached her with a smile, extending his hand. "It's good to see you. You're looking well."

"Thank you," Paige said, shaking his hand.

Bennett scowled at her from the other side of the room.

Paige lifted her chin, determined not to let him rattle her.

Randall Stein strode into the room, a large folder in hand. Samuel's attorney was in his fifties and dressed in an expensive tailored suit. His air of competence put Paige at ease.

How she wished Bennett had stayed home, but he continued to glare at her.

Was it possible that Bennett had been lurking outside her window the other night? No. That person had lacked Bennett's bulky build. Maybe it had been the intruder from the basement.

"Thank you for coming," Randall stated, sweeping out his hand. "Please take a seat." He scanned the room, then focused on Paige. "Will Charlie be here?"

"I thought so," she said, "but I haven't spoken to him today."

"Charlie?" Bennett snapped. "It's bad enough *she's* here. Why would the maintenance man be welcome?"

Paige pressed her lips together.

Randall ignored the outburst. "We need to get started."

They all sat down, spreading out around the long table, which was fine by Paige. Still, she could feel Bennett's stare on her, even from across the table.

Randall began the reading, addressing the distant relatives assembled and what Samuel had left them. Then he addressed Mason. "Samuel wanted to thank you for all your years of working with him. He left you his classic Cadillac convertible."

A burst of love spread through Paige. How like Samuel to think of others in such a generous fashion.

Mason seemed surprised as well. Paige was certain she saw moisture glistening in his eyes.

"'To my nephew, Bennett Calhoun, I leave the sum needed to pay off the debt he has incurred over the years,'" Randall continued. "'I always wanted to help you, no matter your personal opinion of me.' Mr. Calhoun, you and I will discuss those numbers in private."

Paige cautiously peeked at Bennett. The man's complexion had grown dangerously red.

"What about Poinciana Arms?" Bennett demanded.

"Please let me continue," Randall said smoothly.

Randall's composure impressed Paige. She wouldn't have been as calm or firm in the face of Bennett's wrath.

"Since Charlie isn't here, I'll contact him at a later date." Randall smiled at Paige. "'To Paige Meyers, my dear friend and the one person who loves Poinciana Arms as much as I do, I leave all legal holdings to the building, property, and all my personal belongings at Poinciana Arms.'"

A stunned silence fell over the room.

Paige leaned forward, unable to speak. Samuel had left her Poinciana Arms?

Bennett surged from his chair. “This is outrageous. I demand you do something about it right now.”

Randall folded his hands on the table. “I have delivered Samuel’s wishes. That’s all I’m required to do. If you have an issue with his last testament, I suggest you follow legal protocol to address the matter.”

Bennett began to shout about his rights.

The man’s tirade made Paige nervous. She stood and moved farther away from him and closer to the attorney.

Mason jumped up, placing a restraining hand on Bennett’s arm. “Stop. You need to leave.”

“I want answers,” Bennett snarled.

Mason dragged him from the room.

“I’m sorry about that,” Randall said to Paige. “Are you all right?”

Swallowing hard, Paige smoothed her jacket with shaky fingers. “It’s not unexpected.”

“Still, Bennett should have been able to control himself,” Randall said.

She placed a hand on the table to steady herself. “Samuel really left me Poinciana Arms?”

“He did.”

“But why?”

He smiled. “He told me that he was impressed with how you carried out your duties there. The longer you managed the property, he saw that not only were you more than competent at the job, but you had a true love for the place and the people who live there, exactly as he did.”

Paige felt tears forming, and she wiped them away.

“You were wonderful with the tenants and came up with inventive ideas to streamline the running of the complex,” Randall continued. “Samuel couldn’t imagine leaving the destiny of Poinciana Arms in better hands. He felt safe leaving his legacy to you.”

Her entire body trembled. "I don't know what to say."

He laughed. "Samuel knew you'd have this reaction." He shifted papers around in the folder, removed an envelope tucked in the back, and handed it to her. "This is for you."

Paige went teary again when she recognized Samuel's handwriting on the crisp white envelope.

"Everything you need to know is written in his own hand," Randall added.

She nodded, her throat tight.

"I imagine you'll want to read the letter in private," he said. "This has been a surprise, so I suggest we meet again in a few days to go over the legal matters of the ownership transfer. That should give you time to let it sink in."

"Thank you." Paige slid the envelope into her purse and left the room. As she exited the building, her mind darted in many directions. The contents of the will were even more surprising than she'd imagined.

Before she reached her car, Mason stopped her.

Paige pulled her purse over her chest like defensive armor and looked around for Bennett. Was he waiting for her out here?

"Don't worry," he said. "Bennett left."

She sighed in relief.

"I'm sorry he upset you. He wasn't exactly gracious."

"I guess I don't blame him," Paige said. "He's so sure the property should be his."

"Be that as it may, he should have handled the situation better," Mason continued. "If you want, I can still work with perspective buyers." He pulled some papers from a binder. "I've worked up some numbers and—"

She held up her hand. "I appreciate your work, but can we please put this on hold?"

"Of course." He backed off. "You need to do some thinking."

Actually, Paige didn't have to think about selling the building. She knew that Samuel had never wanted to sell Poinciana Arms, and she planned to honor his wishes.

"We can always discuss—"

A ringing came from her purse, interrupting the accountant.

"Please hold on." She pulled out her phone. Charlie's name came across the caller ID. "Where are you?"

"My truck broke down," Charlie said over the loud noise in the background. He gave her the address. "Can you pick me up?"

"Of course. I'll be right there." Paige hung up, then turned to Mason. "I'm sorry, but I need to run."

"I understand." He removed a business card from the binder and handed it to her. "You can reach me here."

After sliding the card into her purse, Paige hurried to her car, driving on autopilot in Charlie's direction. Her mind refused to accept the reality of Samuel's bequest. Was it really true that she owned Poinciana Arms?

Once she arrived at the intersection, she didn't see the handyman's old, battered truck. Where was Charlie? Had he given her the wrong address? She parked in a nearby lot, got out, and walked to the sidewalk, pulling out her phone to tap his number.

The call went straight to voice mail, and she left a message. "I'm here. Where are you?"

Paige rested one hand on her hip, the other hand shielding her eyes from the noon sun, as she scanned the street. She walked the block, but there was still no sign of Charlie. Veering in the opposite direction, she started to cross the street.

Suddenly, a car sped up, heading straight for her.

Paige froze.

A split second before the car hit her, she came to her senses and flung herself to the sidewalk. The air from the moving car brushed across her legs. She tripped, falling to her hands and knees on the hot concrete, her phone flying out of her hand.

The car continued down the street, tires screeching as it swerved out of sight.

Paige pulled herself up, her heart racing out of control. Her palms and knees were scraped. Her hair had escaped the confines of the style she'd corralled it into earlier. Adrenaline and the rapid pace of her heart were all that kept her upright. Had a car nearly hit her?

Unfocused and in shock, she tried to work through her cloudy impressions of what had happened. Strident voices forced her back to reality. She went stiff, in defensive mode, as a young man ran in her direction.

"Ma'am, are you okay?" he asked, helping Paige to her feet.

"I-I'm not sure."

The man pushed his sunglasses on top of his head. "I called the police."

"You didn't have to," she said. "It was an accident."

"That's not what it looked like to me. That car tried to run you down." He gestured to her leg. "You're bleeding."

Paige glanced down. At the sight of the trail of blood, she felt her sight swim for a second until she pulled herself together.

Sirens in the distance grew closer, and soon a police officer and two paramedics rushed over to her.

"Are you hurt?" one of the paramedics asked her.

"No, I'm fine," Paige said. "Just a few scrapes."

"We should examine you anyway," the other paramedic said. "It's better to be safe than sorry."

"I have some questions for you when you're done," the officer said to Paige. He walked over to the young man who had helped Paige earlier.

The paramedics examined Paige and bandaged her up. Fortunately, her injuries were minor, and she didn't need to go to the hospital. She thanked them before they left.

The police officer returned, and Paige explained what had happened.

"The man who witnessed the incident didn't get the license plate number," the officer said. "But he did give me a make and color of the vehicle."

Still fuzzy, she asked, "Is that enough to find who did this?"

"We'll check into it, but it would have helped if we had a number," the officer said. "I'll check the traffic cameras." He gave her his information and told her where she could get the report. "Is there anyone I can call for you?"

Paige felt utterly alone. Her family lived states away. Lexi sat in a school classroom. Samuel was gone. "I'm fine. Thank you."

He nodded and strode back to the squad car.

The young bystander joined Paige. "Are you sure you're all right?"

"Yes, I'm fine," she said. "Thank you."

He nodded, then wished her well and walked away.

Once the man was gone, her knees started shaking.

Paige searched for her phone. The sunlight shining off the screen pinpointed its location a few feet away in the grass. Making her way in that direction, she hissed out a breath as her legs trembled. Thankfully, the device hadn't sustained damage, so she pulled up the only number she could think of.

"There's been an accident," she said without preamble.

"Are you okay?" Jason asked, obviously concerned.

To her dismay, she burst into tears. "Not really."

"Where are you?" After Paige gave him the location, he said, "I'll be right there."

The drive seemed to take forever. All kinds of horrible thoughts ran through Jason's mind as he struggled through heavy traffic. His racing heart slowed a fraction when he finally glimpsed Paige seated in the grass under a tree.

When she spotted him, she rose and tucked strands of hair behind her ear.

He parked and rushed over to her, embracing her as tightly as he dared without hurting her. "Are you injured?"

"Mainly rattled," Paige said.

Jason stepped back and looked her up and down. Anger swelled when he noticed the bandages on her palms and knees. He fought through the rage until he could finally speak. "What happened?"

She took a shaky breath. "A car nearly hit me." She went on to explain Charlie's phone call.

His concern grew as he processed the story. Why had Charlie called Paige to pick him up when he wasn't even here? Had he lured her to this spot? But why? Jason pushed aside his suspicions and focused on Paige. "You're sure you don't need to go to the hospital?"

"I'm sure. The paramedics already examined me," Paige said. "I'll be okay."

"Let's get your things. Then I'll drive you home." Jason didn't give Paige a chance to argue. He put his arm around her shoulders and led her to her car.

After she retrieved her purse, he ushered her to his car and got her settled in the passenger seat. They were quiet as he drove to Poinciana Arms.

"Thanks for coming," Paige said, breaking the silence. "I didn't mean to bother you."

Jason tightened his grip on the steering wheel. She'd nearly been hit by a car, and she was worried about him? "You know I'm always available to help," he told her in a mild tone, despite the hammering in his chest. "I'll come back and get your car later."

She stared out the window. "I appreciate it."

They arrived at the building, and he escorted Paige to her apartment. When she rolled her eyes at him, he knew she'd had enough of his solicitousness.

Jason raised his hands. "I can't change who I am."

"I'd never ask you to."

A hush permeated the apartment when they entered. He knew Lexi wouldn't be home from school for a while yet, so he planned on sticking around to make sure Paige was all right.

Paige limped to the couch and gingerly sat down, leaning her head on a pillow.

"Do you have any pain reliever?"

She motioned toward the kitchen. "Cabinet by the sink. Second shelf."

Jason found the bottle and filled a glass with water. After returning to the living room and handing her the medicine and the glass, he took a seat at the end of the couch, giving her plenty of room.

Paige shook out two pills and swallowed them, then studied his face. "What are you thinking?"

"First of all, where was Charlie?"

"That's the weird thing. He gave me the address, yet I couldn't find him." She sat up. "Do you think he lured me there?"

"It had crossed my mind," he admitted.

"And he never made it to the lawyer's office for the reading of the will."

"Oh, how did that go?"

"You'll never believe it," Paige said. "Samuel left me Poinciana Arms."

Jason gaped at her, speechless.

She grinned. "Yeah, that was my reaction too. Samuel willed me the building, the property, and all his personal belongings. I considered him my friend, but I never expected that he'd leave me his legacy."

"I never met the man, but I can see why. You love this place. Probably as much as he did."

Her lips trembled. "There are so many questions I want to ask him, but now I can't."

"It's the hardest part about being the one left behind."

Paige rested a hand on his arm. "Alyssa?"

He nodded, tamping down the heartache of his old wound. "But life goes on."

"In my mind I understand that, but it's another story for my heart." She stared at the floor. "I don't want Lexi to know about the accident."

"She's going to have questions when she sees the bandages," Jason pointed out.

"I'll tell her I tripped," Paige said. "I don't want to worry her, especially since we don't know what actually happened."

"We do know. A car tried to run you down."

"Maybe I wasn't paying enough attention before crossing the street."

"I don't believe that," he said, "and I know you don't either."

"True," she said. "But I'm not telling Lexi. Please don't mention it to her."

"It's your call." Jason gazed into the distance as a heavy silence descended on the room. A door slammed in the breezeway. Voices grew louder, then softer as people passed by. When he checked Paige again, her eyelids had drooped. Apparently, the adrenaline was wearing off.

He let Paige sleep, easing off the couch to avoid disturbing her. He paced, his mind running through scenarios. He kept coming back to one in particular. Bennett was searching for papers that he claimed proved his rightful ownership of Poinciana Arms. Would he stop looking for them now that Paige had been named the legal owner? Probably not. If anything, he'd be even more determined. So what did that mean for Paige?

And why try to run her down on the street? She hadn't previously planned to pick up Charlie, so no one else knew where she'd be. Jason couldn't discount her feelings of being watched. Had someone followed her and decided on the spur of the moment to take her out? Had Charlie set her up?

The background checks had come back today. He'd had a chance to pore over the information, but it hadn't been deep enough to give him any real leads. Nothing that could pinpoint a reason for Charlie to be after Paige. So Jason had initiated a deeper check with a rush on it.

Thirty minutes passed before Paige stirred. She shifted, then slowly rose up on her elbows to take in her surroundings. She saw him and sent him a sleepy smile.

The sight stole his breath. Jason hadn't considered the possibility that his life would change when he moved into the apartment next door, but it had. Significantly.

"Sorry. I didn't mean to doze off." She swung her feet to the floor and winced.

"You'll need to take it easy for the next few days."

"I don't imagine climbing stairs is going to feel great." Paige stood. "I'm going to change." She took her time hobbling to her room.

A key sounded in the lock, and Lexi breezed in. She frowned when she saw him. "Where's my mom?"

"In her bedroom," Jason answered.

"What are you doing here?" she snapped as she dropped her backpack on the floor.

"Your mom had an incident and called me."

Lexi's eyes went wide. "Incident? What does that mean? What did you—"

Paige came into the room, pulling her hair into a loose bun. She'd changed into yoga pants that covered her knees and a long-sleeved shirt that hid the bandages on her palms. "You're home. How was school?"

Lexi charged over to her mother. "Jason said you had an incident."

Paige reached out to smooth her daughter's hair. "I fell in a parking lot and skinned up my knees."

"So why is he here?" Lexi demanded.

Jason walked over to them. "I was visiting until you came home from school."

Lexi sent him a glower that said she didn't believe him, but she didn't argue either.

"Since I'm not going to be up to much today, I think I'll go through Samuel's boxes," Paige said to Jason. "They're mine now, so I need to decide what to do with Samuel's memories."

"Hopefully, it'll take your mind off earlier events." He hadn't found anything of interest when he went through the contents, but he imagined Paige had the same hope that they would discover a clue.

"Is that what Samuel left you?" Lexi asked her mom. "The stuff from the basement?"

"A little more than that," Paige said. "He left me Poinciana Arms."

Lexi blinked, confused. "Poinciana Arms? Like, *this* Poinciana Arms?"

"The one and only," Paige said with a smile.

"Wait," Lexi said. "He left you the building?"

"And the property," Paige added. "What do you think?"

"Poinciana Arms is ours?" Lexi asked, beaming.

Paige laughed. "Yes."

Lexi flung her arms around her mother. "I can't believe it. I never imagined anything so amazing." She stepped back. "So now what?"

"We celebrate Samuel," Paige said softly.

Lexi nodded and hugged her mom again.

Jason watched mother and daughter as they discussed the news, sure Paige hadn't put two and two together. The stakes had risen, but they weren't in her favor.

"Do you mind if I go over to Tina's?" Lexi asked her mom. "I can't wait to tell her."

"As long as you stop for takeout on the way home." Paige retrieved money from her purse and gave it to Lexi.

"I'll be back soon," Lexi said. She rushed out of the apartment.

Paige stared at the door, obviously lost in thought.

Jason moved closer. "I could have picked up dinner."

"Thank you, but you've done more than enough already," she said. "Besides, I want to start cataloging Samuel's belongings."

"Are you all right?" he asked, studying her.

"I'm in shock about the inheritance," Paige replied. "But if I had a choice, I'd rather have Samuel here with us."

"I'm sorry," Jason said. He wished he could take away her grief and protect her from harm. Today's events had shaken him to the core.

He cared about Paige, and he realized it was impossible to deny his growing feelings for her. "I wanted to tell you—"

A pounding on the door interrupted him, followed by incensed shouting. "Open up! I know you're in there!"

Paige jumped. "That sounds like Bennett."

Jason stepped in front of her. "It's time we officially met," he said, then swung the door open.

Bennett stood on the other side, disheveled and angry. "I want those papers."

"You need to leave," Jason said, his tone icy.

Bennett tilted his head back to meet Jason's glare with one of his own. "I don't have anything to say to you."

"Well, I have plenty to say to you," Jason said. "Leave Paige alone."

"Not until she gives me those papers." Bennett peered over Jason's shoulder and glared at her, his eyes unfocused. "This property is rightfully mine."

Paige remained silent, and her legs started to tremble.

"Call the police," Jason told her quietly.

Paige hurried to the phone, dialed 911, and took the handset to the small foyer, where she could monitor the altercation.

"Go ahead and call the police," Bennett said. "I'll tell them you stole my birthright."

A dispatcher answered the call, and Paige told her what was going on and requested police assistance.

"Back off," Jason warned Bennett.

The irate man raised his eyebrows. "Or what?"

Jason took a step toward him, and Bennett moved away.

"The police are on the way," Paige informed them as she stood glued to the floor.

Bennett seemed to sag under some invisible weight. "You must have the papers," he pleaded but with less steam than before. "I can't find them anywhere else."

"I don't have any papers." Paige inched closer. "And I didn't know Samuel's intentions for Poinciana Arms."

"Samuel robbed me of my inheritance," Bennett insisted.

"I don't think he did," she said, keeping her tone soft.

"You thought he was a great man," Bennett spat. "But he treated me like a poor relation and never helped me. Now I'll take back all that is mine."

Paige doubted his words. Samuel had told her many times that he'd tried to help Bennett, but his nephew always refused. Bennett had been troubled, and he was never content with what he had.

A siren sounded in the distance, drawing closer.

"This isn't over," Bennett threatened, then fled into the courtyard.

Jason started to follow.

But Paige grabbed his arm. "Let the police handle him."

"He might get away."

"If he does, they'll find him after we file a report. He's not going far. Not if he thinks I have the papers."

Jason gave in, but his tense muscles told Paige he didn't like it.

Two uniformed officers entered the courtyard. "Ms. Meyers?" one called.

Paige slipped by Jason to meet them. "That's me. I made the call." She noted their name tags that read *Edgar Green* and *Melinda Davis*.

"Where's the disturbance?" Officer Green asked.

"It was right here," Paige said, motioning to her apartment. "But the man who caused it took off when he heard the siren."

After Jason described Bennett's car, Officer Green strode toward the sidewalk and the street beyond.

Paige told Officer Davis about Bennett's surprise visit.

The officer took notes. "Has he threatened you before today?"

"Yes, but I didn't take him seriously," Paige admitted. "But now, I can't take any more chances. I have a teenage daughter to keep safe."

When Officer Davis had finished asking Paige questions, she interviewed Jason.

Jason gave short and direct answers. He also described the car incident, which Paige had left out.

The officer raised an eyebrow at her, then jotted down more notes.

Officer Green returned. "I couldn't find any sign of the man you described."

"We'll continue to investigate," Officer Davis assured them. She handed Paige a card. "Be sure to contact me if you remember anything else."

Paige and Jason thanked the officers, and they left.

"I think a week on a desert island would be the perfect way to settle my nerves," Paige joked as they walked back to her apartment.

Jason followed her inside. "I don't like the thought of you and Lexi all alone."

"I doubt Bennett is going to confront me again."

"He's acting erratically," he said. "You don't know what he'll do."

"Did you see his expression when he talked about the papers?" she asked. "I'm not convinced he thinks they're here."

"But you don't know that for sure."

"So what are you proposing?" Paige put her hands on her hips. "Are you going to camp outside my door for the duration?"

His face became stony. "If I have to."

"That's not feasible."

"At least tell Lexi what's going on so she can be prepared for any possible danger," Jason said. "You need to be honest with her."

"I appreciate your concern, but my decision about my daughter is mine," she said firmly. "Let me handle it."

His phone rang. Blowing out a breath, he checked the number. "I'm sorry, but I need to take this."

Paige nodded. She decided to work off the last of her nervous energy by tidying up the kitchen. Her knees burned as she walked the short distance. While she rinsed the sink and placed a few glasses in the dishwasher, she watched Jason as he paced the living room. His clipped stride didn't bode well to the topic of his conversation.

When Jason hung up, he joined Paige in the kitchen.

"Work?" she asked.

He shook his head. "We have a few things to discuss before Lexi comes home."

She tossed the dish towel over her shoulder. "We just—"

"It's not about your daughter."

Paige went still.

"Let's sit down."

She followed him to the couch, bracing herself for bad news. When she bent her knees, her abraded skin burned. She tried to hide the automatic flinch by bunching up the dish towel and gripping it.

"That was my boss," Jason explained. "He briefed me on what deep background checks returned on Bennett and Charlie."

Paige clutched the dish towel tighter. "Deep?"

"The first report had basic details, but it wasn't exhaustive enough, so I ordered extended background searches."

Unease swam through her. "I'm guessing by your expression that I'd rather not know."

"First of all, Bennett is in major debt," he said. "He hasn't held a steady job in years."

"That confirms what Samuel told me. And why he left Bennett the money to cover his debts."

"His father filed a lawsuit against Samuel on behalf of Bennett's mother," Jason said. "The report states the case was recently dropped."

"Recently?" Paige asked. "Samuel never mentioned it."

"Perhaps he didn't want to worry you. Or maybe he doubted the validity of the claim."

"So what is Bennett up to? He must have suspected Samuel might not leave Poinciana Arms to him. He went on about how those papers would be his proof in case he didn't inherit."

"At this point, there's no telling what he's thinking," he responded. "But he's desperate. And desperate men do desperate things."

She shuddered. "What did you learn about Charlie?"

"He has a police record," Jason answered. "It's sealed, so I don't know the charges."

"I can't believe it," Paige said, her mind whirling. "But the crime couldn't have been serious."

"We can't be sure."

She shook her head, adamant. "Samuel never would have hired Charlie if he'd committed a serious crime. There's no way he would have allowed a dangerous man around Lexi and me."

Jason remained quiet.

"You don't understand," Paige persisted. "Samuel always helped people. I have to believe that no matter what Charlie did, Samuel helped him."

But what about their signals getting crossed today? A miscommunication or more? And why had Samuel kept her in the dark about so many things?

"Maybe it's time to talk to Charlie," Jason suggested.

"I agree. The sooner the better."

"There's one more thing."

She groaned. "Oh no."

"To cover all the bases, I also did a little digging on Mason Trembly," he said. "His accounting firm is legitimate. However, he has a footprint in the real estate market."

"That would explain why he wants to sell this property."

"He doesn't have a real estate license. At least, nothing on record. Instead, he seems to facilitate the sales through his firm."

"Can he do that?" Paige asked.

"I suppose if he's working with a licensed broker," Jason answered. "I investigated the sales he's connected with. They're all high-end properties located in the immediate area."

"That must be why Samuel wanted to make Poinciana Arms a landmark—to keep others from pressuring him to sell his property."

"That would make sense."

She clasped her hands in her lap. "Wow, that's a lot to process."

"I know," he said. "Now you can see why I didn't want to bother you."

"I'm glad you did. It helps to know what's going on."

Jason gave her a pointed look.

Paige realized that her comment also applied to her daughter. "Okay, I see what you mean. I need to be honest with Lexi too."

"So you'll be more cautious?" he asked. "Not take anyone or anything for granted?"

"I promise," she said, then shook her head. "Who knew my new neighbor would turn out to be so bossy?"

Jason chuckled. "I never guessed my new neighbor would be knee-deep in danger."

Paige blew out a breath. "Should I send Lexi to her dad's?"

"Are you seriously asking my opinion on your daughter now?"

"Yes."

"I think it might be best until we know what's going on."

She stood and limped to the window. She would own Poinciana Arms soon, so she no longer had to fear losing her job. But she still had plenty of other worries. The threats from Bennett. Trying to figure out Charlie's intentions. If she did call Kevin, would all this be a valid reason for him to fight for a legal change of custody? For Lexi's safety, would Paige take that chance?

Jason came up behind her. "You have some heavy-duty thinking to do."

"It seems to be the assignment of the day." Paige lifted her chin. "I will make the best choices."

"I know you will."

They stared at each other for several seconds. If this had been a romance movie, they would have shared a kiss, regardless of the danger. But this was real life, not wishful thinking.

He finally said goodbye and left the apartment.

Paige walked around to get rid of the nervous energy, but it hurt. She remembered the four boxes in the utility room and decided on a distraction. She found her keys and went outside, ready to dig into Samuel's treasures.

A smile that felt out of place with everything going on curved her lips when she thought about examining Samuel's belongings and recalling the stories of each piece. At least she still had those mementos to hold on to.

When Paige arrived at the utility room, she noticed the door was ajar. Her heart rate kicked up a notch. Had someone broken in?

She cautiously approached the door and peeked inside. It was too dark to see anything from where she was, so she crept closer.

Suddenly, there was a loud clatter, and something shot out the door.

Paige almost fell backward. She steadied herself against the doorframe and took a deep breath.

Then Paige felt something rub against her ankles, and she yelped before she recognized Gus. "You scared me to death," she admonished the cat.

Gus spotted a squirrel and took off in pursuit.

Paige opened the door wider and entered the utility room. The first thing she noticed was a broom on the floor. Gus had probably knocked it over, and the clattering noise had frightened him so he'd fled the room. She laughed at the realization that the terrifying intruder she'd imagined had turned out to be a cat.

She scanned the rest of the room and saw only three boxes on the floor. Jason said he'd delivered the boxes. Why was one missing? She quickly rummaged through them and found that the collection of odds and ends was gone.

Paige checked the lock on the door. Sure enough, there were scratches around the wood, and it was splintered in places. Who had broken in?

Her first thought was Bennett. He had been empty-handed when he came to her door and screamed about his rightful legacy. Could he have broken in here first, taken the box, then come back to throw them off his trail?

But how would Bennett have known about the boxes, much less where Paige had stored them? Or maybe he'd broken into the utility room to snoop around and decided the contents of the box were worth money. Either way, this theft had Bennett written all over it.

She returned to her apartment as quickly as her banged-up knees would allow and retrieved the card Officer Davis had given her.

The officer answered on the third ring.

"This is Paige Meyers. You took a call at Poinciana Arms a short while ago."

"I recall," Officer Davis said. "Has the situation changed?"

"Yes. I went to one of our utility rooms after you left, and the door was open. A box that was stored there is gone."

"We'll be right there," the officer said.

Paige moved into the courtyard. As she waited, she gazed at Jason's door. It took everything in her not to go over, but hadn't she bothered him enough for one day? For one week? Paige had gotten used to handling all aspects of her life alone. Until Jason came along, she'd never thought she needed another person to be a sounding board, a protector, or a friend. Jason fit all three. Again, the same question troubled her. Once this was over, who would Jason be to her?

The officers arrived once more, and Paige led them directly to the utility room.

"Are you sure the room was broken into?" Officer Green asked.

She showed them the jimmied lock and cracked wood.

The two officers exchanged glances before moving inside.

Davis studied the room. "Where was the box?"

"Stacked with the others, I think," Paige said. "My neighbor brought them in."

Davis raised an eyebrow at her. "So you didn't actually see the boxes after your neighbor made the delivery?"

"Well, no, but Jason wouldn't take anything," Paige replied. "He's been sort of watching out for me and my daughter."

"What's your neighbor's apartment number?" Green asked.

Paige told him, then added, "But he's been helping me."

Green nodded, then swiftly exited the room.

She wondered if he was going to question Jason. She made herself draw in a calm breath. "I think Bennett Calhoun took the box. He's been hanging around the complex, searching for something he claims belongs to him."

"We'll check him out," Davis assured her.

What more could Paige do? She hated feeling so helpless.

The officer regarded her. "Anything else you want to tell me?"

Paige immediately thought of Charlie. He'd been acting unusual, but was it enough for her to throw him under the bus? No, she wouldn't do that until they talked. "Nothing else."

Davis walked out of the room and gestured to the door. "You'll probably want to get that lock replaced tomorrow."

Paige followed, then started toward her apartment. Jason stood at his door, the late afternoon light bathing his handsome features.

When he noticed her, emotion was erased from his features—no understanding, no questions, no affection. Did he think she'd called the police on him?

Before Paige could go to Jason and explain, Lexi rushed over to her, eyes wide with alarm. She held two takeout bags, and her sparkly mini backpack draped over her shoulders. "Mom, what's going on?"

The officers stopped to check in with Paige one more time before leaving.

It didn't escape Paige's notice that Jason's door was closed, as if he'd closed her out. Her heart squeezed.

"What's going on?" Lexi repeated.

Paige focused on her daughter. "Let's go inside."

As soon as they entered the apartment, Lexi dumped the bags on the counter and whirled around. "Why were the police talking to you? It's Jason, isn't it?"

Paige reared back. "Why would you ask that?"

"The police were talking to him, and I thought maybe he broke the law."

"No, this isn't about Jason. For the record, he hasn't done anything illegal." Paige couldn't decide how to break the news, so she plunged ahead. "There's been a bit of a situation going on around here."

Lexi shrugged off her backpack and tossed it beside the bags. The key hanging from the zipper banged on the counter. "What kind of situation?"

"Let's sit down," Paige suggested.

When they were seated on the couch, Paige rolled her shoulders, then told Lexi everything that had happened since the day of Samuel's funeral. About being watched, possible intruders, run-ins with Bennett and his conviction that Poinciana Arms should belong to him. The near miss at the street crossing. How Jason had been helping Paige the whole time.

The color drained from Lexi's face. "Are you okay?"

"I'm fine," Paige said. "Don't worry about me."

"Why didn't you tell me?" Lexi asked.

"I'm sorry," Paige said. "I didn't want to worry you. But things seem to be getting worse, and you should know the truth."

"Mrs. Nelson mentioned that she thought some of her collection had been moved around in her apartment, but I laughed her off," Lexi said. "I can't believe someone broke into her apartment. I thought we were safe here."

"We both did." Paige took a deep breath. It was time to be proactive. "Have you seen any strangers hanging around? Maybe some kids from school?"

"What?" Lexi demanded, outrage tinging her voice. "You think my friends and I would actually break into people's apartments?"

"I didn't mean to—"

"How could you?" Lexi interrupted. The pitch of her voice went higher. "Do you think *I'm* a thief?"

"No, I . . ." Paige decided to be completely honest with her daughter. "You have to admit, you've been awfully distant lately. And on top of that, you have expensive shoes and a dye job that I know costs more than your allowance or babysitting Muffin."

Lexi pouted. "You think I stole stuff to get money?"

"I don't want to."

A nerve-racking silence sucked the air from the room.

"It's Dad," Lexi blurted out.

"What are you talking about?" Paige asked, confused.

"Dad sends me extra money. He said it should stay between us."

Paige was stunned. She'd never expected this. "Why would you keep that from me?"

Lexi stared at her feet. "Because you're all about being independent from Dad. You don't want his help. He sends me money so I can get the things—" She stopped abruptly.

"That I won't get you," Paige finished for her.

Guilt flushed Lexi's cheeks.

Paige rubbed her temples. "We are on totally different pages."

"I didn't mean to keep this from you," Lexi said, "but it's between Dad and me."

Paige rubbed a hand over her heart. The secrecy hurt. She'd been so worried about possibly losing her job and how that might affect the custody arrangement that she'd never considered that her daughter and ex-husband were purposely keeping her out of the loop. Had Paige been that hard on Lexi? Had she made Lexi think Paige couldn't afford the things Lexi wanted? She'd been trying to teach her daughter lessons that Kevin had completely undermined.

"I'm sorry," Paige said, reaching out and touching her daughter's shoulder. "I shouldn't have assumed the worst."

"And I should have been honest." Lexi shifted her weight. "It's just that since the divorce, I've felt torn between you and Dad."

"I get it. And I'm not opposed to your father giving you money, but I'm not happy that you were keeping it secret."

"I didn't like it, but Dad thought it was best."

Paige wasn't surprised. Kevin had never liked her boundaries with Lexi. "You know I'll need to discuss this with him."

Misery etched Lexi's face, but she nodded.

"I don't want any tension between us," Paige said. "Do you want to tell me anything else?"

"There is one more thing."

Paige wondered what else there could possibly be. Bracing herself, she asked, "What is it?"

"Remember the day we were cleaning out Samuel's storage unit?" Lexi asked. "I sort of took some of his things."

Paige opened her mouth, but no words came out.

"I'm sorry." Her expression fell. "Jason already told you, right?"

"What do you mean?"

"He saw me do it. I was sure he'd rat me out."

Jason knew all this time that Lexi had taken some of Samuel's belongings and hadn't told her? The sense of betrayal swept over Paige again. Why hadn't Jason said anything, especially when she'd told him that she was concerned about Lexi's behavior?

"No, he didn't say a word," Paige said coldly.

Lexi's eyes went round. "I figured he'd tell you right away to get points."

"Points for what?"

"You know, so you'd date him."

"Jason and I are not dating." Paige didn't know what they were, but dating didn't fall into the realm of possibility right now. Not if he was already hiding things about her daughter from her.

Lexi didn't respond.

Shaking off her scattered emotions, Paige said, "I'm glad we had this talk. I need you to promise you'll be careful when you walk to school or hang out with your friends." She paused. "Maybe you should go stay with your dad until things calm down."

Lexi wrapped her arms around her middle. "You're scaring me."

"I don't mean to," Paige said, "but this is serious."

"It's almost the end of the school year," Lexi reminded her. "I have finals. Can't it wait?"

"Going away might be for the best."

"I promise I'll be careful."

Paige considered her request. As much as she desired her daughter's safety, she didn't want Lexi far away from her. They'd handle the situation. "Okay, you can stay for now." She sighed. "I suppose we should try to eat."

"I'm not really hungry," Lexi said.

When Paige opened the bag, the aroma of the Chinese food made her stomach flip over. Her appetite fled, although she did feel better that she'd told Lexi the truth about the strange happenings around Poinciana Arms. Despite her arguing the point with Jason, Paige agreed that Lexi needed to know the truth in order to take necessary precautions. But the rest?

Paige knew the lingering jitters would keep her from settling down this evening. She wanted to march over and confront Jason.

But she feared that would only make things worse.

A soft rap on the door pulled Jason from his thoughts as he sat before his computer screen. He opened the door, surprised to see Paige on the other side. "Checking to make sure the police didn't cart me away?"

She had the grace to blush. "I'm sorry about the police questioning you. But your name came up because you were the last one to see the missing box."

"Now I'm on their radar." Jason was annoyed that the police suspected him of stealing the box, but what bothered him even more was that Paige hadn't come to him first. Hadn't he proven she could trust him?

"I'm sure they don't think you had anything to do with the theft," Paige assured him.

He frowned. "No, but if there are new complaints of missing belongings, I'll be the first person they'll interrogate."

"I hope not." She paused. "So why didn't you tell me that Lexi had taken some of Samuel's things the day we cleaned out his storage unit?"

Jason should have informed her, but he'd let his uncertainty make the decision for him. The irritation on her features told him he was going to pay for it. Whatever trust he'd hoped for had gone up in smoke because of his choice. "I wanted to give her the benefit of the doubt."

"She's my daughter," Paige said. "I should have known."

"I agree, but you made it clear that you and her dad were handling it. Who am I to interfere?"

Her expression turned contrite.

"And to be honest, I began keeping an eye on both of you because of all the unsettling events around here," he said. "From the day I moved in, there have been issues."

Paige stared at him. "You've been watching us?"

"That didn't come out right," Jason answered. "What I meant is, I wanted a handle on the circumstances. Then we started becoming more involved in the mystery and things started getting out of hand. I was hoping Lexi would come forward on her own."

She rubbed her forehead. "After all you went through with your sister, why couldn't you be honest with me?"

"You said you'd handle it with your ex and that it was an issue for her parents."

An awkward silence descended.

"Now what?" Paige asked. "Where do we go from here?"

"Why can't things remain the same?"

"You withheld something important from me," she said, "and I can't have that in my life. If you weren't honest about Lexi, what else would you keep from me?"

"Other than making the wrong decision to remain silent, I've never kept anything from you," he insisted.

"I need to go." She took a step back, then started walking away.

Jason kicked himself for not trusting his gut. He shouldn't have held back the truth from her. Where did that leave them now? He shut the door behind him and jogged to catch up to her.

"I need to make my rounds," Paige said. "I don't need your company."

"Well, I'm not leaving."

In silence, they checked out the laundry room, where she switched off the lights.

As they continued on, he asked, "Do you do this every night?"

"What? My job?"

When they got to the basement door, Jason noticed that Paige shivered.

She unlocked the door, approached the alarm keypad, and stopped. "Someone left the lights on down here too."

He followed her down the stairs.

"I don't need you interfering," Paige called over her shoulder.

"You may be angry at me, but it doesn't mean I'm going to fall down on *my* job."

At the bottom of the stairs, she faced him, hands on her hips. "Your job?"

"Making sure you and Lexi are okay."

A flush crept into her cheeks.

Jason peered over her shoulder and noticed a pile of rubble on the floor. He moved around her for a better view. "Look."

Paige joined him, and her gasp echoed off the walls.

Around Samuel's storage unit, the concrete had been chipped and small sections of the wall had been punched out. Against the wall sat a very familiar yellow toolbox, with a myriad of tools scattered on the floor.

"Charlie's toolbox," she whispered.

Jason crouched down to examine the disturbed area. Chips of concrete littered the floor, disturbing the dirt beneath. "He was digging for something."

"No, this can't be right." Paige shook her head. "Charlie came into the office last week with a brand-new toolbox."

He stood. "Why did he buy a new toolbox when he's clearly still using this one?"

She wrapped her arms around herself. "He said sometimes you have to go for a change, but I thought it was odd."

Jason studied the damage, thinking hard. "The haphazard way the wall and floor have been disturbed bothers me. Someone is getting desperate in their search." He gazed solemnly at her. "And given everything that's already happened, I'm afraid of what they'll do next."

The next morning, Paige entered the office, eyes red and scratchy, head pounding, knees and palms aching. She'd managed to pull on a button-down shirt and a pair of baggy slacks—not exactly professional, but the outfit would pass for today. She clutched a hot cup of coffee, hoping the caffeine would clear out the cobwebs. So far, no luck.

Taking a seat behind her desk, Paige called the answering service and retrieved the messages she had missed after powering off her cell phone last night. She'd had enough pressure building on her. Taking calls didn't usually stress her out, but it had felt like one thing too many with the other blows coming in from all sides. As the night slipped into morning, the weight of owning Poinciana Arms terrified her. What had Samuel been thinking when he willed it to her?

Unable to sleep, she'd read Samuel's letter in the dim hours of the morning. She'd been putting it off, afraid of something she couldn't define. Maybe she feared his written words were the final goodbye. Her fingers had trembled as she unfolded the paper.

Dear Paige,

I'm sure my decision to leave you Poinciana Arms comes as a surprise, but it shouldn't. From the day you took the job as manager, you've loved the building and the people as much as I have. You have become the heart and soul of the place.

You're probably starting to second-guess yourself. Don't. You are the right person to take over Poinciana Arms. Aside from your immaculate management skills, I've always admired your strength, your love for Lexi, and your unwavering loyalty as a friend. You are like a daughter to me.

She had wept silently as she read Samuel's words. Her chest grew tight. If she thought she'd made any progress in healing, it all fell apart as she continued.

I'm sorry I didn't inform you of my plans. You would have argued with me, even though it would have gotten you nowhere. You know that when my mind is made up, there's no changing it.

Please don't waste your years being sad over me. I want you to live a happy life. You certainly made mine special in the short time we spent together.

Samuel

Paige had leaned back against the pillows and grieved until the sun came up, then washed her face to get ready for the day. Samuel had faith in her. It was about time she had some in herself.

Now she had five messages from tenants with one issue or another. Thirty minutes later, she'd scheduled times to check out the apartments and decide what needed to be done about a leaky toilet, a dishwasher on the fritz, and Mrs. Nelson inquiring who would watch Muffin while she attended her volunteer meetings if Lexi got the job she'd applied for.

Paige took a drink of coffee and called Charlie. It went straight to voice mail. Frustrated, she left a message for him to call her back. He had work—and some explaining—to do. Then she lowered her forehead to her desk and counted to ten.

Her cell phone rang, and she checked the screen. It was Mason.

"Good morning," he said pleasantly when she answered. "I hope I'm not calling too early."

"Of course not," Paige said. She didn't mention that there was no such thing as too early when she'd been up almost all night. "What can I do for you?"

"I wanted to know if you're ready to discuss the purchase proposals I mentioned. Poinciana Arms is a hot commodity, and it will go quickly in today's market."

She massaged her temples. "To be honest, I haven't given any thought to selling the property."

"I don't want to add any undue pressure, but you don't want to miss out," he said. "Surely you realize what a gift this is."

Indeed she did. It was a gift from the man who'd wanted Poinciana Arms to be preserved, not sold to the highest bidder. "As you can imagine, I have a lot on my plate right now."

"I do sympathize," Mason said, compassion in his tone. "But it's my duty to remind you that this deal won't last long before the buyers move on."

Even though Paige had already decided not to sell, she didn't want to flat-out refuse the offer. Mason was being supportive and patient, and he thought he was watching out for her best interests. "Can you give me a little more time to think things through?"

"I don't want to pressure you, so let's try for a happy medium," he answered. "Let's talk it over next week."

"That sounds good," Paige said. "Thank you."

"If you need anything, please don't hesitate to ask," Mason said.

After she disconnected, she filled out some paperwork and made a few more calls.

An hour later, Paige still hadn't heard from Charlie, so she dragged herself, knees still stinging, to the apartments to talk to the tenants with the problems. Soon she had a to-do list for Charlie. She'd need to consider hiring a new handyman if Charlie didn't get his act together soon. Samuel had likely hired him for a good reason, and Paige sympathized with Charlie's grief. But her tenants—yes, hers—deserved reliable care, and Paige had to put their needs first.

Paige ate a light lunch at her desk, replaying her earlier conversation with Mason. His helpfulness was the one area in this entire mess that seemed normal. Why not sit down with the man and thank him for his concern? It was the least she could do.

She fished Mason's business card from her purse and read the address. She'd never needed to go to the accountant's office before. Normally, she sent him the information he needed, or he stopped by the complex for specific paperwork. It wasn't a familiar part of town, but on a whim, she decided to drop in. If she found him, they could also discuss why she didn't want to sell Poinciana Arms.

Paige collected her keys and purse and walked to her car in the parking lot. Jason had retrieved it for her last evening.

Fifteen minutes later, she parked by a run-down strip mall that contained a combination of offices and small stores. She hadn't quite expected the tired air of the place.

After checking the number on the business card, Paige exited the car and walked to Mason's office. *Prospect Management* was stenciled on the window in chipped and faded letters. Was it the name of his accounting company? She referred to the card again. It only had Mason's name, phone number, and this address.

Paige stepped closer and cupped her hands around her eyes to peer inside. In the dim lighting, she could make out a few empty desks. Another held a landline phone and a calculator beside a stack of papers. She spotted a couple of filing cabinets and a doorway to another office.

Curious, she went to the front door, but when she pulled on the handle, it remained shut. She tugged once more, but it didn't budge.

When Paige returned to the window, she noticed movement in the back room. Someone searched a desk, banging the drawers in the process. She tapped on the window, but the person stepped out of view. Frustrated, she knocked harder.

The person walked over to the window and saw her.

It was Charlie.

He gaped at her, then spun around and ducked into the other room.

"Charlie!" she called out as she knocked on the window.

One of the neighbors poked his head out the door of the next office. "Can I help you?"

Paige forced a smile. "No thank you. I think this door is stuck, so I'll try around back."

She hurried around the building, wincing from the pain in her banged-up knees, and found an empty alley. She counted doors until she came to the office space where she'd seen Charlie. She yanked on the door, and it swung open. Without hesitation, she rushed inside the office, nearly running into Charlie.

"What are you doing here?" she asked.

"You need to leave right now," he growled.

Paige crossed her arms over her chest. "Not until you explain what's going on."

"I can't."

"Or you won't?"

Charlie sighed. "It's complicated."

"Are you in trouble?" she asked. "Tell me what is, and we can work it out."

"It's not what you think."

"I don't know what to think," Paige said, throwing up her hands.

"Please leave," he begged.

She raised her chin. "No."

Charlie shook his head. "I'm sorry," he said, then stalked to the back door.

"You're leaving without an explanation?" Paige called out. "This is crazy. Talk to me."

Without another word, he opened the door and disappeared outside.

Paige stared at the door, then glanced around Mason's office. There had to be a good reason why she'd found Charlie here in a completely empty office on a weekday. But she had no idea what it could possibly be.

Paige made her way to the front sidewalk and entered the small appliance repair shop next to Mason's office.

The same man who'd spoken to her stood at the counter, screwdriver in hand. "Didn't find what you were looking for?"

"No. But I can't help wondering why my friend gave me this address if his office is unoccupied."

"Next door? He's been in and out for months, and he never stays very long. I've seen him with a few clients, but not nearly as many as you'd expect."

"Thanks," Paige said. Retracing her steps, she stopped at each of the stores in the building, asking about Mason.

The other occupants rarely saw him or didn't know him at all.

What kind of an accountant didn't keep regular hours? Maybe he worked from home. That would explain the empty office but not Charlie searching the place.

What had Charlie gotten mixed up in? Paige tried not to worry, but she had a dreadful feeling that something horrible was about to happen.

Jason sat on the bench in the courtyard, hoping to catch Charlie before the handyman left work for the day. He still couldn't come up with a solid reason why Charlie would leave his toolbox in the basement for anyone to find. If Charlie was sneaking around the complex seeking the papers Bennett wanted, he wouldn't leave a trail that led directly to him. No, there had to be a piece of the puzzle missing.

Then there was the situation with Paige. She had every right to be angry with Jason over the situation with Lexi. He could only pray that Paige didn't have it in her to stay mad long.

Time passed. Neighbors came and went, waving at Jason. There was no sign of Charlie or Paige.

Jason texted her and waited. When he didn't receive an answer, he finally retreated to his apartment. Should he let her make the first move? What if she had news about Charlie? It pained him to wait, but how many operations had he toughed out when patience became paramount? He could do this.

At eight thirty that evening, a steady knocking came from his door. Paige stood on the other side. She was pale, and she shifted from foot to foot, her gaze darting around wildly.

"What's wrong?" Jason asked.

"I'm worried about Lexi." Paige hurried inside. "She didn't come home for dinner. I've been calling her phone, but it goes straight to voice mail."

His senses went on high alert. "When did you talk to her last?"

"This morning when she left for school."

"Could she be with friends?"

"That's possible," she admitted, "but it's not like her to ignore my calls, no matter how upset she is with me."

Jason had seen the two of them together, and while they'd been at odds recently, he believed her. "Where does she like to hang out?"

"The park." Alarm sharpened her tone. "With a group of friends I don't know."

His gut told him that the time for sitting and waiting was over. They needed to move—and fast. "Then let's go over and check it out in person."

"You wouldn't mind?"

"Of course not," he said. "Last I checked you weren't happy with me, but this is more important than a disagreement."

Her mouth tightened. "I can't worry about us until I know Lexi is okay."

Jason wondered if she realized that she'd referred to them as "us." But he wouldn't forget.

When they arrived at the park, Paige tried calling and texting Lexi again, but she didn't respond.

They walked around, but they didn't see Lexi anywhere. Tourists were leaving restaurants, and shopkeepers were closing their establishments for the night.

"I don't see her," Paige fretted.

"Let's check the marina," Jason suggested, leading the way.

The sound of laughter filled the air.

Paige increased her pace and rushed over to a group of teenagers. She called out to a young woman with long brown hair, dressed in the same fashion Lexi favored. "Tina?"

"Hi." Tina glanced around. "Where's Lexi?"

"That's what I came to ask you," Paige said.

Tina wrinkled her forehead. "Why would you ask me?"

"She's not home, and I haven't heard from her all day," Paige replied. "Did you see her after school?"

"At the last bell, we agreed to meet here after school let out, but she never showed." Tina shrugged. "I figured she went home."

Paige grabbed Jason's arm in a death grip. Fear poured off her in waves.

Jason realized he had to take control of the situation for Paige's sake. He introduced himself to Tina and asked, "Are you sure Lexi planned to come here?"

"Yeah," Tina said. "She told me she'd heard from her dad and they were planning their summer trip. She wanted to tell me about it."

Paige leaned against him.

Jason put his arm around Paige to keep her steady. He asked Tina, "Did she say anything about making any stops after school?"

Tina shook her head, her expression growing nervous. "She hasn't returned my texts either."

By this time, the rest of the kids had stopped talking and stood behind Tina, reacting in varying degrees of interest.

"I saw her go into the dollar store," a boy with shaggy hair said. "She waved."

"Did anyone else see her?" Jason asked, scanning the group.

The teens shook their heads.

"What's going on?" Tina asked.

"I don't know," Paige said, then stared at Jason as if he had all the answers.

While he appreciated her belief in him, he was as stumped as she was. "Thanks for your help," he told the teens.

"If you see Lexi," Paige said, her voice trembling, "please ask her to call me."

Tina promised to do so.

As they walked away, Jason's heart rate skyrocketed. If Lexi hadn't met her friends, where could she be? "Can you think of anywhere else she'd go?"

Paige blinked rapidly.

He stopped and gripped her by the shoulders. "Think. I know you're rattled, but we need to keep our wits about us."

She nodded. "Let's try Mrs. Kelly's antique shop. Maybe Lexi got an answer about her job application."

Three blocks away, they caught the well-dressed owner as she locked the ornate glass door.

"Have you seen Lexi today?" Paige asked Mrs. Kelly.

"No, but I called her after school." Mrs. Kelly smiled. "I offered her the summer job, and she accepted it. I thought she would have told you."

"That's wonderful," Paige said. "I haven't heard from her yet."

Mrs. Kelly's smile faded. "Perhaps she wanted to tell you in person."

Paige's shoulders slumped as Mrs. Kelly wished them well and walked away. They stood on the sidewalk, the clock ticking.

Jason recalled what one of the teens had told them. "What about the dollar store?"

"It's another block over," Paige said, pointing.

They rushed to the store.

An older man stood behind the counter, closing out his register. "Everything okay?" he asked Paige.

"I'm trying to find Lexi," Paige said. "Have you seen her?"

"I saw her a few hours ago." The man lifted his chin. "It was odd. She didn't head out to the marina to meet her friends. I saw her make a right on the next street over and figured she was taking the shortcut back to Poinciana Arms."

"Thank you," Paige said, her voice raspy.

Jason regarded Paige and saw the worry etched on her features. Her eyes were bright, her breathing was unsteady, and her skin had lost its color. "Let's retrace her steps," he said, hoping that once they returned home, they'd find Lexi safe in the apartment.

They left the store and took the shortcut the shopkeeper had indicated. The buildings began to transition from business to residential.

Paige motioned to an alley between two houses. "This way."

In the light from his cell phone flashlight, Jason recognized the looming shape of Poinciana Arms as they drew closer.

Steps before reaching the property, Paige stopped in front of one of the houses. She gasped, then ran a few feet away and knelt down in the grass.

"What is it?" he asked, rushing over to her.

When she stood, she held a pink-and-white sneaker. "It's the same shoe Lexi wore to school today."

After discovering Lexi's sneaker, Paige and Jason immediately called the authorities.

For the third time in the span of a few days, the police arrived at Poinciana Arms. The same officers showed up at Paige's apartment, and she filed an official report.

"We'll start searching for your daughter right away," Officer Green assured her.

Paige nodded. But what if they didn't find Lexi? She tried to calm down, but her anxiety spun out of control, and she felt as if she couldn't catch her breath.

After the officers left, Paige told Jason, "My daughter is missing. I can't sit around and wait. I have to do something."

Jason ran a hand through his hair, as he had at least ten times tonight. "We've already looked for her, and the authorities are on it. If we don't hear anything by morning, I promise we'll try again."

But morning was a long way off, and with each beat of her heart, Paige prayed for Lexi's safety. This had to be a mix-up. Paige kept waiting for Lexi to breeze through the door and say, "You'll never believe what happened."

Except Paige could only imagine the worst.

"Thank you for being here," Paige said softly. "It helps not to be alone."

"I wish I could do more."

"You've already done so much."

The minutes dragged on, and Paige finally talked Jason into

cruising the neighborhood. They had found Lexi's shoe. Surely, they'd discover another lead.

They drove around for hours, but they came up empty. They were no closer to finding Lexi than before. Paige could hardly stand it.

Once again, they returned to Paige's apartment. She didn't sleep a wink. Jason stayed with her, and while his mere presence was comforting as usual, her heart could not be soothed this time. He paced the living room and talked on the phone. From the snippets of conversation she heard, she could tell he was speaking to his contacts.

Early the next morning, two different police officers checked in, but they didn't have any news about Lexi. Paige managed to pull herself together enough to be coherent, instead of the mess she'd been hours earlier.

As soon as the officers left and closed the door behind them, Paige collapsed against Jason, feeling numb.

He pulled her close, his arms like a safety net wrapped around her. "I know this is hard, but I promise we'll find her."

Paige nodded against his strong chest and drank in the scent of his woodsy cologne. In his warm embrace, she tried to focus on calming her mind. Finally, she pulled away.

"I'm going to my place to take a shower," Jason said. "I'll be back soon."

"I'll be here," Paige said.

When Jason left, she wandered around the apartment. Eventually, she decided a shower might do her some good too.

As Paige stood under the hot stream of water, her knees trembled, and she released the tears she'd been fighting all night. This was her fault. She'd put her daughter in danger, and now she had no way of helping her. What kind of mother did that? Even though Lexi had refused to go to her dad's, why hadn't Paige insisted? Everything she'd been worried about paled in comparison to the safety of her daughter. If Lexi—

No, she couldn't go there. Another round of sobs hit her. She leaned against the tile wall and went with the wave.

Finally, she cried herself out. Paige washed her face and vowed not to collapse like that again. She had to be strong. Lexi depended on her.

She shut off the now-cold stream, pulled her hair into a ponytail, and dressed in a pair of shorts and a T-shirt.

Suddenly, it hit her. In the fear of losing Lexi, Paige had forgotten about Mason's office and Charlie lurking inside. She hurried into the living room to find Jason sipping a cup of coffee. His hair was damp, and he'd changed into a pair of faded jeans and a button-down shirt.

"I didn't tell you what happened yesterday," she said.

He set the cup down and gave her his full attention.

Paige told him about how nice Mason had been when he'd called. She described how she'd remembered his business card and drove to his office to have a serious conversation about the future of Poinciana Arms, but she'd been caught off guard when she arrived. The office had an air of abandonment, and Charlie had been inside. "There has to be a connection," she reasoned, even if it felt like grasping at straws.

"Maybe," Jason said. "But first let's check the surveillance cameras at the stores Lexi would have passed yesterday. I'm sure the police will review them, but I don't want to wait. It's possible we'll catch something out of the ordinary and piece together a picture of her movements."

Desperate to do something, Paige agreed.

They headed out, stopping at every business Lexi would have passed. The owners of the tight-knit community all knew Paige and Lexi and were eager to assist. In one store, they saw video of Lexi strolling by the window and talking on her phone, a typical happy teen. Was she excited because she'd gotten the job she wanted? Paige had to fight back another swell of emotion.

As they viewed footage from another store, Jason went still. He pointed to a section of the screen. "I've noticed this same pickup in several of the frames that feature Lexi. It can't be a coincidence."

If Paige had been alarmed before, terror overwhelmed her now. She examined the truck. "I'd swear that's Charlie's pickup." She squinted, but she couldn't make out the driver.

"It's possible, but it's a common kind of truck." Jason peered closer. "Why would Charlie follow her?"

"I don't know," she said, shuddering.

At the dollar store, the video showed the same truck, but this time it was stopped out front.

"Is it idling?" Jason asked.

Paige's blood froze as she watched the screen. Lexi exited the store and headed for the shortcut to Poinciana Arms. The truck eased into traffic, following her until she moved out of sight.

Jason reviewed the tape once more, then paused it. This time he asked the man behind the counter for a piece of paper.

"What are you doing?" Paige asked.

"I can see a few numbers on the license plate." Jason stepped away and made a call, giving the person on the other end the numbers and the color and make of the truck. She also heard him ask specifically to check Charlie's vehicle records.

When Jason rejoined her, his face was drawn. "Let's go back to where you found her shoe."

Within minutes, they were searching around the house where Paige had discovered Lexi's sneaker.

A woman came out of the house, garden gloves in hand, wearing a wide-brimmed hat. "Can I help you?"

Paige forced a smile. "Sorry to bother you, but my daughter lost a shoe around here yesterday. I was wondering if you happened to see her." She tugged her phone from her jeans pocket and pulled up a picture of Lexi.

"What a lovely girl," the woman said.

"She is." Paige fought the urge to cry.

The woman tilted her head. "I think I did see her. I walked out to the porch to tend to my plants when I noticed a girl walking by. She had the cutest sparkly backpack."

Paige felt tears blurring her vision, and she impatiently wiped them away.

"A truck pulled up beside her and stopped," the woman continued. "I noticed the window roll down. She went over to talk to the driver."

Was it really Charlie? Paige put her hand to her forehead. She thought she might pass out.

"Did you see who was driving the truck?" Jason asked.

"No, but your daughter carried on a conversation with the driver. I assumed she knew who it was."

"Did she leave after that?" Paige asked.

"I'll admit, I was focused on watering a few plants, but when I glanced up again, the passenger door hung open and your daughter got into the vehicle."

Paige swayed on her feet.

Jason wrapped his arm around her shoulders to hold her upright. "By her own free will?" he asked the woman.

"What an odd question," the woman said.

"Please," Paige implored her, "can you remember if she acted scared?"

The woman lifted her hands. "I'm sorry, but I don't know."

Deep down in her heart of hearts, Paige knew that her daughter had been kidnapped. Without another word, she marched toward Poinciana Arms. She heard Jason thank the woman.

A few moments later, he caught up to Paige.

"Charlie must be working for Bennett," she spat.

"We don't know that for sure."

"Who else has it out for me? Who else would take Lexi?"

"If he has her, why hasn't he called?" Jason asked.

Paige had no idea. But she would find out.

She rounded the building and stalked into the courtyard, where Mrs. Nelson and Muffin were seated on the bench near the fountain.

"I need to speak to you," Mrs. Nelson said to Paige.

"I'm sorry, but I can't talk right now," Paige said. "I have an emergency."

Mrs. Nelson frowned. "What's wrong?"

Paige slowed down. "Lexi is missing."

Mrs. Nelson gasped. "Oh no. What can I do?"

Paige was overwhelmed by Mrs. Nelson's kindness. "Maybe wait to see if she comes back? I'm going to a building I visited yesterday to find answers."

Mrs. Nelson squared her shoulders. "Muffin and I will sit right here until Lexi comes home."

"Thank you." Paige ran to her apartment and snatched up her car keys.

Jason strode in behind her. "Where are you going?"

"To the building I told you about."

"You can't be sure Bennett and Charlie are there. Why would they be if there's no connection?"

She paused as her burst of energy faded. "I don't know what else to do."

"I'll drive you," he said.

His phone rang, and Jason answered it.

Paige held her breath. It seemed like the conversation lasted for an eternity.

He finally hung up and said, "That was my friend Tad. He did a search on the pickup we spotted in the surveillance videos."

"And?" she asked, bracing herself for the worst.

"You were right. It's Charlie's truck."

19

Jason drove as fast as he could without drawing the attention of the police.

"Charlie has to be at the office," Paige said, her voice desperate. "He was hanging around there for a reason."

She pointed out the strip mall, and he pulled into a parking spot. Paige didn't even wait for him to shut off the engine before she was out of the car and running for the door. He sprinted after her, afraid she'd throw herself into a dangerous situation.

Jason reached out and caught her arm. "I understand you're scared and you want to find Lexi, but dashing into the unknown without a plan doesn't work. Trust me. Why don't you let me take the lead on this?"

She bit her lip, clearly unsure. "I'm sorry. You're right."

"Good." He let out the breath he'd been holding, then made himself think as a man trained in security should. "Now show me the office."

Paige led him to the office window.

Jason peered inside. Like Paige had described, the place had an air of abandonment about it. There was no sign of Charlie.

She tugged on the door. "It's locked, like it was yesterday."

He scanned the area, hoping to find a truck. Nothing stood out. This part of town had seen better days. It was the perfect place to hide out. But for what reason? "Are there any other ways to get inside?"

"In the back," Paige said, leading the way.

Once they were at the rear of the building, Jason tried the door. It was locked. Again, there was no truck parked nearby.

She sighed. "I was sure Charlie would be here."

"You had a logical lead."

"But that's not enough," Paige said. "Guessing doesn't help Lexi."

"Let's go back to Poinciana Arms and regroup," he suggested. "Maybe we'll come up with another idea."

The despair on her face squeezed his chest in a viselike grip.

As they walked around the building from the other direction, Jason glanced across the street at an abandoned building that might have been a store at one time. He spied the bed of a pickup, similar to the one they were searching for, tucked around the corner of the building.

His heart pounded. "I think I found the truck," he said quietly.

Paige whirled around, hope in her eyes. "Where?"

He pointed at the truck across the street.

"Do you think it's Charlie's?" she whispered.

"Let's find out."

They crossed the street, Jason in the lead. As they approached the structure, he stopped to peek around the corner. Sure enough, Charlie's pickup was parked next to the building.

Paige gasped behind him.

He placed a finger against his lips.

She nodded, her expression tight, but she didn't appear as frightened as before.

They continued on and located a door. Jason twisted the handle, and it swung open. As they walked into the building, he scanned the area, much as he had when he'd worked on covert operations. His training had prepared him for situations like this. He systematically checked doors, windows, open spaces, anywhere they might be able to maintain the element of surprise.

Jason noticed multiple doors lining the long hallway and figured they had once been offices. He crept forward, alert for anything to confirm they were on the right trail.

As they continued on, he heard a voice coming from the room at the end of the hallway, followed by a crash, as if something had fallen. He froze.

Paige stopped behind him and clutched his shirt.

Jason looked over his shoulder and met her gaze.

When the voice spoke again, she mouthed, "Bennett."

He ushered her into the nearest empty office. "We have the element of surprise, but we need to be smart in case Lexi is in there," he whispered.

"What do you have in mind?"

Jason ran through scenarios in his head. They didn't have any weapons, which was a major strike against them. But he could still work with the surprise factor. "Stay here while I check to see who's in the room."

Paige nodded.

He left the office and inched down the hall, hugging the wall, until he could see inside the large room. Bennett pawed through a box, muttering to himself. Jason's heart nearly stopped when he saw Lexi sitting in a straight-backed chair, her sparkly backpack on the floor beside her. The teenager was zip-tied to the chair and clearly terrified.

Jason silently backtracked and rejoined Paige in the empty office. "Lexi is in there, and Bennett is with her."

"Charlie too?"

"I didn't see him."

She moved toward the room.

Jason grabbed her arm to stop her. "We need to make a plan."

"I have to get my daughter right now," Paige insisted.

"Let's call the police first," Jason advised. He pulled his phone from his back pocket and made the call. As he hung up, a sound came from his right.

Charlie stood in the doorway.

Another crash came from the room. Then they heard Lexi's muffled cry.

Paige shook off Jason's hand and sprinted toward the sound of her daughter's cry. Even though she'd agreed that Jason should take the lead, she couldn't stop herself when she knew her little girl was in danger. She skidded inside the room, her heart pumping fast. Her stomach dropped when she saw Lexi zip-tied to a chair. Her eyes were wide, and she appeared terrified.

Paige ran over to Lexi and hugged her. She never wanted to let her go. Breathing in her daughter's scent, Paige whispered, "Are you okay?"

Lexi nodded.

Paige saw Bennett rise from his crouched position beside the box she recognized as the one taken from Poinciana Arms. The items were scattered on the floor, some as far as the other side of the room as if they had been thrown. Was that the crash she'd heard?

Then Paige noticed Mason, leaning against the far wall. She couldn't believe it. What was Samuel's accountant doing here?

Mason pushed away from the wall and stared at Paige with a sinister glint in his eye. "And here I was beginning to worry you'd never find us. Bennett and I were concerned that we hadn't left enough bread crumbs to lead you here."

Paige's throat went dry, and she couldn't move. Confusion overwhelmed her. Why was Mason looking at her like that? She had known him for years, and he had always been so kind and considerate. Now she began to suspect she had never really known him.

Bennett set a stack of papers and a pen on the nearby table.

"Sign over Poinciana Arms," Mason told Paige. He removed a gun from his pocket and aimed it at Lexi. "Or your daughter will die."

At the sight of a weapon pointed at her daughter, Paige felt the blood drain from her face, making her dizzy. She tried to shake off the sensation. Lexi depended on her staying alert. She had to protect her from Mason and Bennett.

Lexi whimpered, and Paige hugged her more tightly.

"I won't ask you again," Mason snarled at Paige. "Sign over Poinciana Arms to me."

All at once, Jason and Charlie burst into the room, and everything seemed to happen in slow motion. Mason aimed the gun at them, but when they continued to charge toward him, he began to back away in alarm.

He didn't get far. Jason tackled him and wrestled for the gun.

But not before a shot went off.

"Jason!" Paige screamed.

The gun clattered to the floor.

Jason rolled the accountant over, then planted his knee in the middle of Mason's back.

Paige rushed over to Jason, fearing the worst. "Were you hit?"

"No, it was a wide shot," he said. "I'm fine."

Overcome with gratitude, Paige sagged in relief. Neither Jason nor Lexi would be taken from her today.

Jason secured Mason's wrists with a length of rope that was on the floor. Charlie pushed Bennett against the wall, but instead of acting belligerent, Bennett went eerily quiet.

With a shake of her head, as if coming to her senses, Paige ran back to Lexi. "They didn't hurt you, did they?"

"No, but I hated being here all night." She jutted her chin toward Bennett. "Especially when he kept mumbling to himself."

Appalled, Paige asked, "Mason left you alone with him?"

"No, they both took off." Lexi shivered. "It was creepy being here all alone. And as much as I tried, I couldn't get loose."

"Don't worry." Paige placed her palm on Lexi's cheek. "You're safe now. We'll untie you right away."

Charlie made a move toward Lexi.

But Paige blocked him. "You're not getting anywhere near my daughter. Not after everything you've done."

Charlie raised his hands and stepped back. "What do you mean?"

"You kidnapped Lexi," Paige declared.

Charlie blanched. "I would never do that."

"Charlie's on our side," Jason said as he joined them. "We suspected Charlie all along, but before we rushed in here, Charlie told me he'd been working for Samuel. He had nothing to do with abducting Lexi."

"I'm still tied up here," Lexi pointed out.

Charlie tossed a pocketknife to Jason.

Jason caught it, flipped it open, and slit the zip ties.

Lexi stood and fell into Paige's arms. They stood there in a tight embrace. Paige silently thanked God for keeping her daughter safe.

"Let's sit tight," Jason said. "The police are on the way."

Paige nodded as she remembered he'd called them before she'd raced into the room.

Jason retreated to a corner of the room, then took out his phone and made a call.

After Paige ushered Lexi over to an armchair, she faced Mason and Bennett. "I think you two owe us an explanation."

"I knew you wouldn't help, since you were close to Samuel," Bennett said. "So I had to search for my birthright."

"What do you think your birthright is?" Paige asked.

"The papers proving my great-grandfather left Poinciana Arms to my mother," Bennett replied. "I know you have them."

"I don't have the papers," Paige said helplessly. "I don't know how to make you believe it."

"You must have them," Bennett insisted. "We didn't find them anywhere on the property."

"So it was you all along?" Paige asked. "You were the one creeping around Poinciana Arms, lurking outside my apartment, and tearing up the basement?"

"Yes," Bennett said. "I had to find the truth before you took it all away."

Paige wasn't surprised that Bennett was responsible for those things. But she still didn't understand Mason's role. "Why are you here?" she asked him.

"I suspected you wouldn't sell Poinciana Arms," Mason replied. "You're too much like Samuel. On the other hand, Bennett needs the money, which makes him so much easier to manipulate."

Bennett jerked his head toward Mason. "Manipulate?"

"You were easy," Mason scoffed. "As soon as I suggested that you were being cheated out of your birthright, you fell into line. I simply made the endgame seem possible while you did all the work."

"But you were sure I'd get ownership of the apartment building," Bennett said, his voice wavering. "You told me that we were in this together."

"I lied," Mason said in a steely tone. "When Paige inherited Poinciana Arms, I'm afraid I had to change tactics. I no longer needed your help."

"But why take Paige's daughter?" Bennett asked.

"Why do you think?" Mason snapped. "Leverage."

"You thought taking Lexi would change my mind?" Paige asked, stunned.

Mason nodded. "It was my last resort."

Anger surged through Paige, and she gritted her teeth.

"We had already brought the box here to see if any of Bennett's crazy ideas panned out," Mason continued. "There were none. Then fortune smiled on me."

A chill ran down Paige's spine.

"I had an associate watching you and your daughter," Mason said. "Tony borrowed your handyman's truck, hoping to lure her away at an opportune moment. When he saw your daughter walking alone, he simply followed her, then stopped to ask for directions. The dear girl put up quite a fight."

Paige could hardly control her rage, but she knew she had to act calm. The police were coming, and they would arrest Mason. He would be punished for his crimes. She glanced at Lexi and noticed her daughter wiping the tears from her eyes. Paige decided it was time to change the subject, so she asked Mason, "Why did you keep pushing the sale of Poinciana Arms?"

"I have major buyers lined up for that property," Mason said smugly. "Investors who want that prime piece of real estate and are prepared to pay for it. I tried to get Samuel to see reason, but as usual, his stubbornness outweighed his business sense. He didn't want to sell. When I found out he wanted to preserve the property as a landmark, I had to take drastic measures."

"What did you do?"

"Arranged a little car accident."

Paige gasped. "You killed Samuel."

"How could you do that to him?" Charlie demanded. "He was a great man, and he treated you well."

"He refused to cooperate," Mason said with a shrug. "I made plans, and my associate carried them out."

"What plans?" Paige asked.

"I called Samuel to inform him that you needed assistance," Mason answered. "It was the easiest way to lure him to the arranged location for the mysterious hit-and-run accident. My associate excels at his job. After I paid him handsomely, he moved on from Samuel to you."

Paige felt sick. Mason had hired someone to kill Samuel, and he'd tried to do the same to her. She couldn't believe that Mason was so heartless. "What else did you pay this murderer to do?"

Mason chuckled. "Follow you. Break into the apartments. Make threatening phone calls. Cut the wires in the parking lot gate. All to scare you into selling. There was really no other way."

Paige couldn't believe his nonchalant tone. "There are lots of other ways. Like realizing you'd lost and moving on."

"Not in this case," Mason said. "I needed the sale of Poinciana Arms to go through. I invested heavily in the crosstown project." His face twisted in a snarl. "It was the one time I miscalculated a risk."

"The project by the highway that went bankrupt?" Paige asked.

Mason's face slowly went red. "One and the same. So I need the money to get out of that mess. You were all that stood in my way."

"You used me," Bennett said quietly. "You gave me hope that Poinciana Arms would be mine. How could you do that?"

"You wanted it so badly, and I simply played into your delusions," Mason said, his features tight. "I did the research too. If Colin Masters wasn't on the original papers, there would be questions about Samuel's legal ownership. I didn't have time to jump through hoops."

Somewhere in the building, a door banged against a wall. "Police!" Rapid footsteps pounded on the concrete.

"I'll meet them," Charlie said, jogging from the room.

Jason finished his call and joined Paige. "I updated Tad and thanked him for all his help."

"Get me out of these," Mason demanded, glaring at Jason.

"Yeah, I'll get right on that," Jason deadpanned.

As four officers stormed into the room, Paige took Lexi's hand and pulled her out of the way.

Two officers escorted Mason out of the room. The man shouted threats that echoed down the hallway.

The other officers steered Bennett toward the door, but he stopped in front of Paige. "I'm sorry." He closed his eyes. "For everything."

Before she could respond, the officers ushered him away.

Paige tried to feel sorry for him, but she couldn't muster up the sentiment. Not with Lexi still in her arms, reminding Paige of what could have happened, of how she could have lost her little girl. Maybe Paige would try to revisit the idea of forgiveness in the coming months.

Two of the officers returned.

"We need to take your statements," one of them said.

After they'd answered all the officers' questions, Paige pulled Charlie aside. She needed her own answers.

He held up a hand. "I know that I have some explaining to do. I'm sorry for not being honest with you."

"That's what I'm confused about," she said. "What were you doing?"

Charlie frowned. "I told you. My job."

"I'm not accepting that as an excuse," Paige said. "Tell me the truth."

He sighed. "Samuel was concerned that Colin Masters not being on record as a co-owner might cause problems going forward. He knew that both Bishop and Masters had purchased the Poinciana

Arms property together, but when he started the process of having it declared a landmark, he realized he needed paperwork that lined up. He asked me to find the original documents."

"So all the slacking off was because you were also searching for the papers?"

"Yes," Charlie said. "After Samuel died, I knew finding those papers was a life-and-death matter. He told me he was leaving you the property, but he was afraid something would happen to you and Lexi when his will was read. I promised him that I would protect both of you."

She puffed out an agitated breath. "I didn't know whose side you were on. Especially when we found your toolbox in the basement and the floor all torn up. Or when I saw you yesterday at Mason's office."

"I know how this sounds, but someone stole my toolbox," he said. "You have to believe me."

"Mason's associate?" Paige guessed.

"Probably," Charlie replied. "That's why I had the new toolbox. I was embarrassed about losing the original, and I was worried you would suspect me. When the truck was stolen, I couldn't tell you about that either, not without having to explain and putting you in danger." He sent her an imploring look. "I'm sorry I couldn't tell you about Samuel's request. I wanted to keep you out of all this trouble."

"I appreciate your concern, but I wish you'd been straightforward with me," she said. "Did you know the gate had been tampered with?"

"I suspected it," he said. "Then when I saw that the wires had been cut, I thought I'd get around to fixing it before you noticed."

"And the day of the will reading. Why weren't you at the location you told me?"

"I accidentally gave you the wrong address. When I realized my mistake, I tried to call you back, but there was no answer. Later I learned about the near miss at the intersection."

Paige realized that the driver had followed her from the attorney's office. She tried not to let the terror of that moment affect her. She shook her head. "I can't believe it was Mason all this time."

"I'm not surprised," Charlie admitted. "The man wanted blood and money."

"Any idea who his associate is?"

"I might have a lead on Tony. When you caught me at Mason's office, I found a ledger with interesting numbers and initials in it that I thought might come in handy. I swiped it and plan on handing it over to the police. Hopefully, they'll find the guy."

She shivered. "I hate the idea of that man out there somewhere, free to do whatever he pleases."

"If he's smart, he's already moved on from Peters Cove," he reasoned. "But I have faith the police will apprehend him soon."

They stood watching the officers investigate the room for evidence.

She spied Jason out of the corner of her eye, and her heartbeat sped up. Figuring out her feelings for him would be the first item on her list after everything calmed down. Turning back to Charlie, she tried to hide a grin. "And your dislike for Jason?"

He had the courtesy to appear guilty. "I didn't know anything about him. Or how to keep an eye on him without making you suspicious. The more time you two spent together, the more I was concerned he was using you to help Mason somehow."

"Like I told you, he helped me."

"Yeah, I get that now," Charlie said. "There's more you don't know." He went silent, and he furrowed his brow. Finally, he said, "I have a criminal record."

She waited for him to explain.

"I was involved with a bad group when I was a kid. We got caught in an armed robbery. I waited outside and didn't have a weapon, but I was arrested as an accessory. After a good lawyer represented me, the charge was reduced."

"I'm so sorry," Paige said.

"Samuel knew about it," Charlie continued. "He was the first person who ever saw beyond my past. He hired me to be the handyman at Poinciana Arms because he saw potential in me."

She smiled. "I understand a little about that."

"I guess you do." He cleared his throat. "Randall Stein contacted me because I missed the reading of the will. Samuel left me his house."

"That's wonderful," Paige said, her heart warming. She pictured Charlie moving into Samuel's well-maintained bungalow located a few blocks away from Poinciana Arms. "I'm so glad."

"It was more than I ever expected," Charlie said. He sent her a sheepish look. "Do I still have a job?"

"Of course you do." She smiled. "We make a good team. As long as you're honest with me from now on."

"Thank you," he said, sounding relieved. "I won't let you down again."

A thought suddenly occurred to her. "How did you know we were here?"

"I went to the complex, and Mrs. Nelson said you'd run off in a hurry to some building you visited yesterday," Charlie said. "I figured it was Mason's office. I told her my truck had been stolen, and she gave me the keys to her car. I saw you and Jason cross the street when I drove up."

Her chest squeezed tight. "Mrs. Nelson stayed and waited for Lexi. Just like she said she would."

"There are wonderful people living at Poinciana Arms," he reminded her.

"I agree, and Samuel loved them all." Paige swallowed hard. "I miss him."

"Me too," Charlie said, his voice wavering. "But we'll always know how much he cared about us, and we'll do everything we can to honor his memory."

She smiled. "We certainly will."

21

Jason waited for Paige to tie up loose ends with Charlie, relieved that they'd found Lexi and both mother and daughter were safe. The nightmare was finally over, and all he wanted to do was gather Paige in his arms and never let go.

When Paige and Charlie finished their conversation, Charlie said his goodbyes and left.

Paige smiled at Jason.

Jason held out his arms, and Paige stepped right in. She wrapped her arms around his waist and rested her head against his chest as if they embraced like this every day. After a long moment, he pulled away slightly. "Don't ever do that again."

"Do what?" she asked.

"Take off when I have a plan."

"I'm sorry," Paige said. "When I heard Lexi scream, I couldn't stop myself."

"You scared me to death," he said. "But I'm so glad you're both okay."

"Can you guys make up later and help me here?" Lexi called out.

Jason reluctantly let Paige go. He hoped to spend a lot more time with her in his arms in the days to come. He grinned at her and warned in a low voice, "This isn't over."

Paige laughed.

They went over and helped Lexi collect Samuel's belongings. As a team. The three of them together.

Lexi motioned to an old wooden box. "What is that?"

"I'm glad you asked." Paige smiled. "You need to learn all about antiques for your new job."

"How did you know I got the job?" Lexi asked.

"We talked to Mrs. Kelly when we were searching for you," Paige explained. She gave her daughter a hug. "Congratulations. I know you'll do great work."

"Thanks," Lexi said, hugging her back. Then she pulled away and picked up the box. "So what is it?"

"It's a humidor," Paige answered. "Samuel once told me he liked to smoke the occasional cigar."

Lexi jumped up and grabbed her backpack, removing the key hanging on the zipper tab in front.

"What are you doing?" Paige asked.

"The day we went through Samuel's storage closet, I took a key from inside the humidor. I thought it was cool at the time and attached it to my backpack." Lexi fiddled around, then inserted the key into an impression on the side. A compartment opened. She peeked inside, and her face fell. "It's empty."

"Can I see it?" Jason asked, holding out a hand.

Lexi handed him the box.

Jason ran his fingers around the outside, feeling a lip. Then he traced the inside compartment and discovered a small spring. He pressed down, and the bottom of the box dropped free of the hinge that had kept it connected. Papers fluttered to the floor.

Paige retrieved the papers and stood. Shock crossed her lovely features. "Could it be?"

"Let's find out."

He set the humidor on the table while Paige carefully unfolded the papers. Jason was amazed at how well preserved they were.

They all leaned in to read the document. It was a bill of sale made out to both Richard Bishop and Colin Masters.

"I don't believe this," Paige whispered as she scanned the second page. "This is a copy of the record filed with the county. Again in both names." She glanced at him, her eyes round. "Bennett had it wrong all along."

Lexi tapped her foot. "I don't know what those papers mean, but technically, I found them."

"You did." Paige laughed and wrapped an arm around her daughter's shoulders.

Jason took the second page from Paige, then nodded at the box. "The humidor preserved the papers the same way it would work to keep cigars safe, protecting the contents from humidity damage and deterioration from sunlight."

Paige studied the papers in awe. "All this time, the papers were right under Samuel's nose, and he didn't even know it. *We* didn't know it."

Lexi frowned at them. "You guys are going to have to fill me in on what's going on."

An officer returned, ready to take Samuel's belongings into custody.

Paige placed the papers back in the humidor for safekeeping. She handed over the humidor and the key and explained what they'd found.

While her mother took care of their discovery, Lexi hugged her backpack. "You didn't tell Mom what I did. Why?"

"Experience," Jason answered.

"What does that mean?"

He briefly told her about his sister. "I didn't see the same agony in you that I saw in Alyssa. It gave me hope that in time you'd do the right thing."

Lexi grimaced. "Yeah, and then Mom got mad at you."

"It was my fault for not being honest," Jason said.

"I wasn't honest either." Lexi stared at the floor. "So you're going to be hanging around?"

"I hope so." He paused, then took a chance. "Is that all right with you?"

"Yeah, you're okay."

"That's high praise."

Lexi chuckled, then grabbed her mother's hand. "Let's go home." She met Jason's gaze and slowly extended her free hand. "All of us."

His heart glitched, and he hesitated.

Lexi grinned like she had his number—that he was a big softy—and planned on using it against him.

After all they'd been through, Lexi had let Jason in. It felt like a victory. Now he had to convince her amazing mother they were worth taking a chance on.

They hadn't straightened things out since Paige learned that he'd kept the truth about Lexi from her. He'd been upset as well, thinking she'd sent the police after him. He hoped they resolved the stumbling block quickly so they could focus on beginning a relationship.

"And I want my other shoe," Lexi said. "My foot is cold."

Paige smiled as Lexi led the way out the door. Over her shoulder, she mouthed, "Thank you."

Jason grinned, knowing he'd do anything to get in Paige's good graces.

When Paige, Jason, and Lexi walked into the courtyard at Poinciana Arms, Paige let out a contented sigh. The music of the bubbling fountain greeted her like an old friend. They were all finally safe. And they were home.

Paige was overwhelmed with gratitude that her daughter was safe and Mason and Bennett would soon be behind bars. She was relieved to know that Charlie hadn't been doing anything wrong or underhanded. He'd simply been carrying out Samuel's wishes.

And Paige was thankful that Jason had been there for them too. His support and strength had carried her through these dark and terrifying days.

A bark and the click of nails across concrete greeted them as Muffin bounded over and jumped on Lexi.

Lexi laughed and cuddled the dog.

Mrs. Nelson rose from the bench, a smile spreading across her face. "I had no doubt of your return."

Without thinking, Paige hurried over and gave the older woman a big hug.

Mrs. Nelson froze, then hugged her back with just as much gusto.

Muffin barked again.

"She doesn't like to share," Mrs. Nelson said with a watery chuckle.

"Thank you for waiting for us," Paige said. "I can't tell you how much it means to me."

Mrs. Nelson seemed too emotional to respond. She scooped up Muffin, waved at the others, and headed toward the stairs.

As Paige led the way to the apartment, Gus sauntered out of the foliage, staring solemnly up at them.

Paige leaned down to scratch behind his ears. "We're home, buddy. That means dinner for you."

He meowed as if he expected nothing less, and when Paige opened the door, he rushed inside.

Paige followed the cat into the apartment. She watched as Lexi entered and tossed her backpack on the counter. Delighted that her daughter was home, Paige pulled her into another hug.

"Come on," Lexi groaned. "I get that you're relieved, but I'm okay."

"I'm more than relieved. Delirious. Blessed. Overjoyed." Paige laughed when Lexi rolled her eyes. "Should I go on?"

"No," Lexi insisted, but Paige read the pleasure in her daughter's expression.

"Then you can expect lots more hugs," Paige said.

Lexi pretended to shudder. "I'm gonna take a shower."

Paige hugged her again, mostly to prove she could, but this time Lexi didn't complain.

When Paige let go, Lexi raced over to plant a kiss on Jason's cheek, then disappeared into her room.

"What was that all about?" Paige asked.

"Your daughter and I came to an understanding," he replied.

She grinned. "Did you now?"

Jason closed the space between them and pulled her into his arms. Paige wrapped her arms around his waist, squeezing tight.

"I think we need our own understanding as well," he said.

"Do tell."

"First, I'm sorry about keeping Lexi's actions from you. I could use the excuse that I've never had kids, but when you made sure to let me know you and your ex had things under control, I guess I closed down." Jason shook his head. "I could also say I don't know how being a parent works, but that isn't true. I had Alyssa, so I know better. I won't dare put us in that place again."

Paige reached up and brushed her finger over his rough cheek, refusing to temper her racing heart and the joy enveloping her. "This is new ground for both of us."

"I'm crazy about you. I have been since the day I spoke to you outside my apartment when I first moved in."

She leaned back. "You knew that soon?"

He raised his eyebrows. "You didn't?"

"I'm pretty sure I knew when you ran down the basement stairs into the unknown with me," Paige said with a laugh. "Any guy who is willing to protect me is number one in my book."

"Even if you're more than capable of taking care of yourself?"

"Especially because I can." All the jumbled emotions inside her melted away. She couldn't deny that she was falling for this man. "We worked together. There's a truth in that I find incredibly attractive."

"I couldn't agree more."

A thought occurred to her. "And here I worried that I was too much trouble."

Jason grinned. "You're the perfect kind of trouble."

"So you plan to stick around?" Paige asked, holding her breath.

"You have to ask?"

Her nerves stretched taut. "Apparently I do."

He sent her a smile that made her forget to breathe. "You're stuck with me."

Taking a chance, Paige gently brushed her lips over his. When she pulled back, she wondered if this was truly the beginning of something special. "Thank you," she said, her voice cracking. "You were there for me through it all. I don't know how to repay you."

"No need." Jason leaned closer and kissed her tenderly.

This time, the spark of destiny made her shiver with delight. These feelings had snuck up on her during the days of anxiety and tension, but could it be true? Could they have fallen for each other so quickly?

After Paige broke the kiss, she asked, "Are you sure we're not moving too fast?"

He grinned at her without a single worry to mar his expression. "No, it's the right amount of time." He kissed her again.

The sound of the slamming bathroom door pulled them apart.

"I need to get that door replaced soon," she said as she extricated herself from Jason's strong arms. She walked into the kitchen and retrieved two glasses from the cabinet, then filled them with iced tea.

Jason followed her. He accepted a glass and leaned against the counter. "So, you're going to take your rightful place as the proud owner of Poinciana Arms?"

"Do you think I should keep managing this place?" Paige asked, genuinely wanting his opinion.

"I do," he answered, his eyes sparkling. "But most of all, Samuel wanted you to do it. He had faith in you."

Memories of Samuel washed over her. She sent him a silent thank-you. "Yeah, I can do this," she announced to Jason and the world.

"Does this mean I get the boyfriend discount?"

"I'll have to get back to you." Paige laughed, knowing they'd have many long, happy years ahead of them to haggle over the rent at Poinciana Arms.